BRIDE OF THE SLIME MONSTER

CRAIG SHAW GARDNER

D0003379

ACE BOOKS, NEW YORK

This book is an Ace original edition,
and has never been previously published.

BRIDE OF THE SLIME MONSTER

An Ace Book / published by arrangement with
the author

PRINTING HISTORY
Ace edition / April 1990

ISBN: 0-441-07950-4

Ace Books are published by The Berkley Publishing Group,
200 Madison Avenue, New York, New York 10016.
The name ''ACE'' and the ''A'' logo
are trademarks belonging to Charter Communications, Inc.

PRINTED IN THE UNITED STATES OF AMERICA

10 9 8 7 6 5 4 3 2 1

This one is for
Charlie,
a slime monster in his own write.

IN THIS ENTHRALLING EPISODE OF
THE CINEVERSE CYCLE, ROGER GORDON AND
DELORES HAVE SOME CLOSE ENCOUNTERS WITH A WHOLE
NEW CAST OF CHARACTERS, INCLUDING . . .

Dwight the Wonder Dog—"*Everybody* knows Dwight the Wonder Dog . . ."

Officer O'Clanrahan—Women in jeopardy? Wrongs to be righted? They're all just part of a day's work.

Dr. Dee Dee Davenport—This beach bunny and nuclear scientist conducts *her* experiments at the Institute of Very Advanced Science.

Menge the Merciless—An all-new, all-evil, all-*dastardly* villain.

And last but not least . . .

Edward the Misunderstood Slime Monster—Hey, give a guy a break—it's not *easy* being a misunderstood slime monster . . .

DON'T MISS THESE OTHER HILARIOUS SERIES BY CRAIG SHAW GARDNER . . . *THE EBENEZUM TRILOGY* AND *THE BALLAD OF WUNTVOR*

"A lot of fun! I could hardly wait to find out what was going to happen next!"
—**Christopher Stasheff, author of** *The Warlock Insane*

"A delight for all fans of funny fantasy!"
—**Will Shetterly, author of** *Cats Have No Lords*

"A slapstick romp worthy of Laurel & Hardy . . . but I warn you not to read it late at night—the neighbors will call the cops when you laugh down the walls!"
—**Marvin Kaye, author of** *The Incredible Umbrella*

"A bizarre, witty, delightful fairy tale for grown-ups!"
—**Mike Resnick, author of** *Stalking the Unicorn*

◭ 1 ◮
"Flaming Death!"

It was the end of the world.

Flying saucers crashed into the Washington Monument. Skyscrapers caught fire. Jumbo jets crash-landed in Peru. An immense ocean liner, quite possibly the *Titanic*, hit an iceberg and sank majestically. Rome burned while Nero fiddled. It was terrible. And Roger was helpless to stop it.

After that, of course, it got worse.

Newspaper headlines spun toward him, freezing in place with headlines like:

> "ROGER FAILS!"
> "DELORES LOST FOREVER!"
> "DOCTOR DREAD TRIUMPHANT!"
> "CINEVERSE DOOMED!"

And it didn't stop there. If that had been the extent of things, Roger still might have been able to stand it. After all, he had become inured to hardship and surprise through a life working in public relations. But no!

1

There had to be those disembodied voices, didn't there? And what voices! First, there was this maniacal laughter: "Ah hahahaha! Ah hahahaha!"

Roger could imagine the man's bald head, gleaming almost with a light of its own as the man's mouth opened, pencil-thin mustache a-quiver, to pour forth that never-ending stream of triumphant mirth.

"Ah hahahaha! Ah hahahaha!"

That laughter threatened to drive Roger into a frenzy. But the second voice did worse than that.

"Roger," she said, "why did you fail me?"

"Delores!" he called, but she did not answer.

"Roger," she said again, "why did you fail me?"

"I couldn't help it!" he replied. "The ring slipped from my fingers. Big Louie grabbed it from my—"

His voice died as he remembered the last thing he heard as he slipped away from the Cineverse. It had been a gunshot, fired—no doubt—by Doctor Dread or one of his insidious henchpeople. Had that bullet hit someone? What if Roger had escaped, only to have someone else die in his place?

"Roger," Delores asked imploringly, "why did you fail me?"

He tried to think of something else he could say, but realized, before he could open his mouth again, that it was no use. Wherever Delores' voice was coming from, she could not, or would not, hear his answers.

He would not accept this! There must be some way—

"Delores," he whispered desperately.

The other voice answered:

"Ah hahahaha! Ah hahahaha!"

"Roger," Delores' voice followed, "why did you fail me?"

The voices were growing louder, as if they were shouting in his ears:

"Roger? Why did you—ah hahahaha!—why did you

fail—ah hahahaha!—why did you—hahaha—fail—ha-haha—fail fail fail *fail*—''

"No!" Roger clamped his hands over his ears. The voices had become too much for him. He couldn't think. He couldn't talk.

He looked wildly about for help—any sort of help. Delores and the villain were nowhere to be seen. He was surrounded by darkness save for a single, distant point of light. Something moved in that faraway illumination, a tall figure, a dark silhouette against the brilliant background. Roger squinted, trying to make some sense of the distant man's movements. He realized at last that the fellow was smoking a cigar—a cigar that produced blue smoke.

Blue smoke?

That's what he needed to get out of here—the blue smoke of a Captain Crusader Decoder Ring! But his ring was gone. How could he ever find another?

Perhaps, Roger realized, the man with the cigar might have the answer. He'd have to call to the stranger to get his attention. Roger took his hands from his ears so that he could cup them around his mouth.

"Fail!" the first voice screamed.

"Ah hahahaha!" the second voice rejoined.

Somehow, the accusing voices had gotten even louder—almost as if they screamed from somewhere deep within Roger's head. He tried to speak, but his own voice was swallowed up in the others' all-consuming cries. He no longer had any hope of calling to the cigar-smoking stranger.

"Fail!—Ah hahahaha!—Fail!—Ah hahahaha!"

He had no hope of anything.

He fell to his knees, but there was no floor beneath him. He was falling, turning round and round, tumbling head over heels toward a distant, even darker point, so deep and far away that it was totally beyond light, and warmth, and redemption.

And still the voices were with him.

"Fail!"

"No!" Roger screamed over and over again as his body plummeted toward the pit.

"Ah hahahaha!"

"No! No! No! *No!*"

Roger woke up.

He looked around. He was in his own bedroom, in his own bed. Dim light filtered through his venetian blinds, throwing bars of yellow-red across the floor. It must be, he thought, close to sunset.

So he wasn't in the Cineverse. Roger sat up. Had it all been a dream, then? Delores hadn't called to him? He wasn't surrounded by evil laughter, forever falling, forever failing?

It had been awfully vivid for a dream. He remembered so many things, so many places and events, marching by him almost like he was watching a movie. But that was it exactly! For how could he have known, when he first fell in love with Delores, that she was an emissary from another dimension?—a dimension that resembled nothing so much as all those films from the thirties, forties, and fifties—all those movies made before the Change. And how could he imagine that you could only visit that other reality, known as the Cineverse, through the use of a small plastic Captain Crusader Secret Decoder Ring, once given away for free in boxes of Nut Crunchies?

He had found so much in the Cineverse, and so many people who had befriended him. Not only Delores, but Doc, a former town drunk, who—when he stayed moderately sober—was a formidable ally. Then there was Zabana, Prince of the Jungle, and Big Louie, who actually was rather short, a sidekick who always seemed to know what you were going to say next. They had all been there when that gunshot rang out. They had all been alive when Roger had vanished from the Cineverse, menaced by the guns of Doctor Dread and his cohorts. Who could say how many of his friends there were still alive?

It seemed all so fantastic now, back in Roger's bedroom,

just waking from sleep. It was difficult to remember the horror he had once felt, when he learned of Doctor Dread's plans for controlling not only the Cineverse, but the Earth as well.

But there was something about that man in Roger's nightmare—something that Roger swore must be very important. Well, he was in the distance in the nightmare, so maybe—working from dream logic—the blue-smoke stranger wasn't important at all. Then why did Roger's stomach lurch when he thought about the man with the cigar?

He shook his head at the impossibility of it all. So much had happened so quickly to Roger, that—especially now that he was back in his old apartment, tangled in his old bedclothes—it all did seem almost like a dream, like the Cineverse was just some figment of his movie-loving imagination. But where did his dreams end and reality begin?

The phone rang.

"Hello?" Roger said.

"Ah hahahaha," a voice replied. "Ah hahahaha!"

The reality of it all came crashing down around Roger.

"Mengeles!" he screamed into the receiver. "What do you want?"

"Only to gloat, dear boy," Mengeles replied in an oily voice. "But now that we know the truth about each other, perhaps you should call me by my true name—Menge the Merciless!"

Roger almost dropped the phone. How could he have been so blind? As a child, he had watched that evil fiend—with his bald head and pencil-thin mustache—week after week on TV in that old movie serial *Captain Crusader Conquers the Universe*. Each week Menge's twisted plans almost defeated Truth, Justice, and the Universal Way, only to be thwarted at the last instant by Captain Crusader's heroics. And now the evil fiend was here, talking on the phone!

No wonder Roger had always had an odd feeling about the man. Since he had only known Menge the Merciless as his mother's next door neighbor, however, he had never realized the villain's true nature. Roger stared at the receiver in horror. How could he have been such a fool?

"You never had a chance against me, pitiful earthling," Menge gloated. "I'll admit that I've had some trouble in the past, with meddlers like that Captain Crusader! But Doctor Dread's master plan put me beyond that snooping Captain, and every other hero in the Cineverse! Now that I am on Earth, a place where they no longer have heroes, how can I help but triumph?"

"Why, you—" Roger paused, trying to find just the right words. Why couldn't he think of something noble and upright to say that didn't sound foolish at the same time?

Menge interrupted Roger's thoughts. "But enough gloating! It's time to plunder, loot, and destroy! But before I go, I must thank you for the four Captain Crusader Rings. I'm sure they will come in very handy in our conquest of the Cineverse. Ah hahahaha! Ah hahahaha!"

Menge hung up. Roger listened to the dial tone, then replaced his own receiver. Depend on a villain like that, he supposed, to not even say goodbye.

And Menge had mentioned the rings. Not that Roger needed to be reminded. When he was a boy, he had found seven of them in Nut Crunchies boxes, and kept them all these years, stored along with all his other childhood possessions, at his mother's home. Or so he had thought. When he had been told the true significance of the Captain Crusader Decoder Ring, he had returned to his mother's, only to find all his keepsakes moved, and many of them sold! After a frantic search, he had managed to find one of the rings, but the others seemed to have vanished.

Now, of course, he knew where the rings had gone. Menge had stolen them! Roger had foolishly thought them safe in his mother's basement. But Dread's minion had not only absconded with four of the precious plastic circlets— not to mention starting a romance of some sort with Roger's mother—he had moved all of Roger's things into his mother's garage!

Roger told himself to calm down. It was time for thought, not anger. He had lost his first ring. Menge had claimed four others among his belongings. But, years ago, when he was twelve, Roger distinctly remembered saving seven of those cheap plastic objects. That meant there might still be a ring or two left among Roger's boxes. True, they could have been lost or destroyed. The rings, keys to the universe that they were, were nevertheless small and cheaply made; incredibly breakable. Maybe they were gone. But maybe they were somewhere Menge hadn't thought to look.

Roger had to go to that garage as soon as possible, and look for whatever hiding places his twelve-year-old mind might have imagined. Delores and the others were in deadly danger; he had to find that ring now.

But what would he say to his mother? Roger had no time for explanations, especially for something as complicated and unbelievable as the Cineverse!

Then again, why did he have to explain at all? If he simply walked into the garage, without knocking on his mother's door, he wouldn't have to explain anything, would he? It wasn't as if he were stealing anything—whatever pitifully few boxes were left, they were *his* things, after all.

That decided it, then—simple, efficient, and completely free of Mother's lectures about his untidiness and the various women in his life. He'd just have to wait for it to be fully dark. His mother would be watching television, if not asleep. He could be in and out of her garage without her ever knowing he was around.

Yes! The plan was foolproof. Roger was surprised for an instant at his new resolve. A few days ago, he would never have dared to do something like this. But that was before he'd survived the Wild West, braved a primitive jungle, and almost been sacrificed to a volcano god! For good or ill, his experiences in the Cineverse had changed him. He trusted they would pay off in this world as well.

He got out of bed, walked into the kitchen, and methodically began to search the drawers. He knew there was a flashlight in there somewhere.

Roger walked quietly to the door at the side of his mother's garage. He had put on his spare jogging suit, a faded blue with silver stripes down the pants and arms. His newer exercise outfit had been severely damaged by adventures on various movie worlds, but he figured an outfit like this would raise the least suspicion in his mother's suburban neighborhood. Heaven knew, there were joggers up and down these streets at all hours of the day and night.

He tried the door. It opened. His mother never locked it. At least that hadn't changed.

He stepped inside, closing the door behind him. He flicked on the flashlight. The beam wasn't as strong as it could have been, barely piercing the gloom. Maybe, Roger thought, he should have checked the batteries.

His foot hit something, which in turn hit a trash can. Roger froze, but heard no answering noise from his mother's house. His stomach growled. He massaged his sneakered foot. What was his mother doing, leaving noisy metal objects on the floor of the garage? After a moment, he moved even more carefully to the shelves in the back of the garage.

Roger's stomach complained again. How long had it been since he'd had something to eat? The last big meal he'd had was the night before he was to be sacrificed to the Volcano God. He had no idea how long ago that was—time in the Cineverse wasn't like time on Earth; on movie worlds there were all these jump cuts. Roger could taste the saliva in the back of his throat. If only he had a little something to munch on. . . .

There was something in the pocket of his jogging suit. Roger fished it out and shined the flashlight beam on what he'd found: a packet of chewing gum with one stick left. Well, it was better than nothing. He unwrapped the stick

and popped it in his mouth. Besides, maybe chewing on
some gum would calm his nerves.

He turned his light to the storage shelves, and almost
immediately found the boxes he was searching for, all
stacked neatly on the uppermost shelf. Menge the Merciless
might have been a scourge and a villain, but at least he was
tidy.

Roger set about methodically exploring the half dozen
boxes still left from his childhood, doing his best to keep
quiet. The first held only elementary school papers and
projects, the second various broken toys he'd been unable
to part with. The third box was a bit larger and more interesting. It contained half a dozen figures left over from
his Zorro fort, his incomplete set of "Mars Attacks Earth"
cards—he was missing Number 22—and a catcher's mitt,
which Roger's father had bought in the forlorn hope that
his son might take up baseball. Roger smiled when he
thought of his father's impossible quest. After all, who
needed to take up sports when there were so many good
comic books and movies around? Roger hadn't really discovered exercise until sometime after he discovered girls.
Except for one or two halfhearted games of catch begun in
their backyard on his father's insistence, this glove had never
been used.

Except—

Roger's heart threatened to beat its way out of his chest.
After he'd given up his brief baseball career, this glove had
been virtually useless, *except as a place to hide things*.
Small things in particular—small, round, cheap plastic
things, like Captain Crusader Decoder Rings!

Roger quickly reached inside the glove, and felt the piece
of tissue paper he knew would be there. Perhaps he got a
bit too excited, or pulled the paper free a bit too rapidly.
Whatever the reason, he lost his grip on the box. It fell to
the cement floor with a dull thud. Roger hoped it was too
soft a noise for anybody to hear. He pulled the tissue paper
from the ring. Yes! He didn't even have to shine the flash-

light on it. He'd know the feel of this cheap plastic anywhere.

It was a genuine (accept no substitutes) Captain Crusader
Decoder Ring!

That's when he heard voices. His fingers went numb.
The ring slipped from his hand.

The voices were coming from outside the garage. Roger
turned off his flashlight. He strained to hear the words.

"Now, I might just be a foolish old lady, but I swear I
heard something."

It was his mother's voice! Roger had to do something!
His foot hit the box on the floor. It produced a sound that
was much louder than he might have liked.

"See, Mr. M? I told you I heard something in the garage."

Mr. M? But that was his mother's pet name for the man
who was actually Menge the Merciless!

"Don't worry, Mrs. G," Menge replied smoothly. "I'm
sure it's only a raccoon or some other lowly beast. I shall
dispatch it handily."

"A raccoon?" his mother said distractedly. "Oh my. I
don't think I could watch."

A motor rumbled to life. The garage door was opening,
revealing two silhouettes, a man and a woman, on the other
side.

"I certainly understand, Mrs. G. I wouldn't want to of-
fend your delicate sensibility. Lucky for both of us that I
thought to bring my gun."

Roger saw that the silhouette of the man held the silhouette of a very large revolver. The second silhouette looked
an awful lot like a Magnum.

"You're such a gentleman, Mr. M. Then, if you'll excuse
me?"

"Yes, certainly, Mrs. G. Feel free to go into the house.
I'll let you know when it is all over."

This was terrible! Roger had to find that ring and get out
of there. Where could that ring have gone?

Something went *crunch* under his sneaker. Roger felt where his foot had been, and found four small pieces of plastic. He looked up as he stuffed them in his pocket.

His mother had disappeared into the house. Menge turned on the overhead light. He smiled at Roger.

"This is even better than I thought," the villain gloated once again. "Ah hahahaha. Ah hahahaha."

"Oh no, you don't!" Roger retorted, figuring that was the sort of thing you said to an archvillain.

Menge continued to grin.

Oh no, don't you? Roger thought. What had he meant by that?

"I'll call my mother!" Roger added a second later.

Menge hefted his Magnum meaningfully. "And I'll shoot you with this. It's a shame that I couldn't see who you were in the dark. A tragedy."

Roger recognized a threat when he heard it, especially when that threat was spoken by a man with a pencil-thin mustache.

"What do you want from me?" Roger asked.

"I think you and I are going on a little trip." Menge waved his gun at the open garage door. "At least, that's the way my boss, Doctor Dread, would put it."

Roger walked out of the garage, followed closely by Menge and his gun.

"Next door," Menge instructed. Roger did as he was told. Menge steered him into another garage. The merciless one waved his gun at a red sports car.

"I realized," the villain continued, "after I spoke to you on the phone, that it might not be enough to simply deny you the use of a ring. You've been to the Cineverse, after all, and it was possible that a little bit of that place's heroics had rubbed off on you. So I figured it was time to make some contingency plans. Plans that have to do with your death. If you'll climb in the car?"

Roger felt the gun's cold steel against his cheek. He climbed into the driver's seat.

"And put on the seat belt." Menge instructed.

Roger clicked the belt in place.

"You'll find that seat belt has some amusing properties." Menge's pencil-thin mustache quivered upwards. "I have made some modifications in it, you see. Once closed, the belt cannot be taken off. The clasp is permanently locked." The gun muzzle gently caressed the car's door frame. "I have made other modifications to this vehicle as well, such as the removal of the brakes, and certain adjustments to the gas tank to assure that, if you hit something, it will explode." He reached across Roger and turned the key that was already in the ignition. "It is, of course, providentially coincidental that your mother and I live at the top of a hill and the road down ends in a cliff."

Providentially coincidental? Roger had always thought of that particular cliff as "picturesque." He knew now that the cliff would mean something much more final to him very shortly.

"Oh," Menge added cheerily, "I forgot to tell you about the automatic acceleration valve—" A red light blinked on in the middle of the dashboard. The car's lights turned themselves on. The horn beeped merrily.

"—but I don't think we have any more time for conversation," Menge shouted over the racing engine. "I don't think we have time for any more than a *bon voyage*!"

The car started by itself with a squeal of rubber, its wheels gaining speed as it rolled down the driveway and the road beyond. Roger tried to turn the steering wheel, but it was locked as well.

"Ah hahahaha!" he heard behind him. "Ah hahahaha!"

The car went faster still. It sped past the stop sign, and across the main road. There was the hard crash of rending metal as the car broke through the roadside barrier and went hurtling out into space. For a single, quiet moment, Roger felt weightless, suspended in midair. Then he, and the tons of metal surrounding him, began their descent.

He stared through the windshield. Now that the sports

car was pointed straight down, Roger could see his destination, some hundreds of deadly feet away.

The car was falling to the rocks far below, and certain, fiery death!

⟁ 2 ⟁
"Murder by Slime!"

Roger was never around when she needed him.

Delores would have felt more put out had she not been staring down the barrel of a gun. Of course, it was hard to blame Roger. She really hadn't gotten around to explaining exactly who she was when the two of them had gotten involved. Or the exact nature of the Cineverse. Or what would happen if you dropped a Captain Crusader Decoder Ring when you were right in the middle of using it. Or much of anything, actually.

She sighed. They never told her it would be this difficult when she was in Hero School. Then again, when she went to Earth to look for help in her fight, she never realized she might fall in love.

"All right!" Big Bertha barked in her ear. "No looking wistful over there! It is not the proper response to half a dozen villains threatening you with high-tech weaponry. We expect fear, trembling, useless pleas for mercy—that sort of thing. Getting a faraway look in your eyes like that is asking for trouble!"

The smile faded from Delores' perfect lips. She defiantly tossed back her long blond hair. They wanted her to play by their rules, did they? Well, she had some rules of her own—and Delores played for keeps!

She stared back at Bertha, the only woman she knew who could wear a festive island muumuu and make it look like a set of combat fatigues. She, and five assorted male lowlifes, all pointed guns at Delores and her allies. A couple of the lowlifes attempted to leer in her direction, but they were forced to look away when she gave them one of her practiced, withering glances. Even Big Bertha took that moment to examine her Uzi automatic more closely. The only one not affected by Delores' stare was their leader— who stood behind the others, and a bit to one side—the insidious Doctor Dread, dressed once again in his signature pale-green metallic snakeskin suit. He held no weapon himself, preferring to merely smile evilly in the background.

So Delores and her allies were slightly outnumbered. Still, there was no fear in her heroic heart.

At least the islanders had excused themselves when the battle between the forces of Dread and Delores had gotten serious, so that the locals could, as their elder proclaimed, "pursue their peaceful native existence." That meant Delores didn't have to worry about hurting any innocent bystanders. In other words, her hero gloves were off.

She glanced for a final time at her three companions. They were not without their resources.

Zabana, Prince of the Jungle, stared stoically at their enemies. He pointedly ignored the livid red scar that crossed his left cheek, a scar made by a bullet intended for Roger.

"Flesh wound," the blond giant announced when he noticed Delores examining the scar. "Zabana laughs at flesh wounds!" He turned back to stare at the enemy, absently flexing his pectorals.

"We'll give them more than flesh woundsh!" Doc croaked from where he sprawled atop the igneous rock. His hands groped toward his twin, pearl-handled revolvers, both still in their holsters. "Now, where did I put my gunsh?"

Delores glanced next at the shortest of her three fellows, Big Louie. Louie grinned back and tipped his hat. Delores bit the corner of her perfect lip with one perfect tooth. She had some trouble with Big Louie. Zabana and Doc were both heroes, in their way, and Delores knew she could count on both of them, within certain limits. Big Louie, though, was a sidekick. Delores admitted it; she was always a little uncomfortable around sidekicks. She could never quite figure out what they did. She wondered now just how Big Louie fit into all of this.

"I'd wonder about that, too," Louie answered, although Delores couldn't remember voicing her question. "I guess, one way or another, I move the plot along."

Move the plot along? Delores frowned. Is that what happened with the bullet and the ring and Roger's disappearance? It was all so confusing. What was happening to the Cineverse, anyway?

But then she realized that this confusion was what it was all about—Doctor Dread's evil plans, Roger's disappearance, her rescue mission, their search for Captain Crusader, everything! Ever since the Change had ripped through the movie worlds—when heroes started to die, lovers weren't always united, masked killers continually came back from the dead, and the villains often won—there had been something wrong with the Cineverse. But the Change had been too unstable.

Now, the Cineverse was changing again. And Doctor Dread wanted it changed his way.

"There she goes," Big Bertha hissed, "wandering off again into one of those explanatory asides. I don't think she takes our threat seriously!"

Doctor Dread cleared his throat delicately.

"Perhaps," he said unctuously, "we should show them"—he paused knowingly—"the meaning of the word."

Bertha clicked off the safety on her weapon.

"Machine guns," Zabana said derisively. "Zabana laughs at machine guns!"

But Delores wasn't laughing. She was thinking of escape. Dread and his cohorts had backed them up against the live volcano, quieter now that it had received its sacrifice of assorted bad guys, but still deadly if they were to step back into its steaming maw. There had to be some other way out of here!

They would already have escaped, if Dread hadn't so quickly brought back those five other henchpeople to replace the ones he'd lost in the volcano. It had been very confusing there in the moments after Roger's disappearance, and Dread had become very speedy with reinforcements and costume changes. Delores sometimes wondered where the criminal genius found all those lackeys.

"Central casting," Louie replied, even though Delores still couldn't remember speaking. "But I have an idea."

"Enough"—Dread paused purposefully—"shilly-shallying! We will show these upstarts what it means to cross the next"—he hesitated meaningfully—"ruler of the Cineverse!"

The five other lowlifes all cocked their various weapons. If they were going to escape, Delores realized, it had better be now. Louie had said he had an idea? Of course! Roger had disappeared when Louie grabbed the ring. And that meant—

"Zabana! Doc!" Delores called. "Grab hold of Louie. Louie, take out that ring!"

"That's what I—" Louie began.

"They're going to escape!" Big Bertha cried out.

Delores clamped her hand on Louie's shoulder.

"Twist that sucker!" she ordered.

"But—" Louie began.

"Deal with them!" Dread ordered.

Six bad guys pulled their triggers. Louie grabbed the ring and twisted. The four of them were surrounded by blue smoke as half a dozen shots rang out.

• • •

Delores blinked as the smoke cleared.

"Valerie!" a man shouted.

"Kenneth!" the woman replied.

They had landed in a very well-appointed drawing room.

"Oh, if I had but known what your sister really meant!" Kenneth exclaimed.

"Poor, deluded Daphne," Valerie agreed. "But she knew her love was hopeless, even then!"

"Yes," Kenneth insisted, "but with a man who may be destined someday to be prime minister—"

Delores frowned. Where had the decoder ring landed them? She glanced at her three companions, but they looked as confused as she. Louie had turned the ring so quickly, he would have had no time to choose a destination. Wherever they were, they seemed to be out of any immediate danger. But they would have to know in exactly what sort of a world they had landed in order to chart an intelligent course out of this place, a course through which they might find Roger, or even Captain Crusader!

"I'm sorry," Valerie was saying, "but I feared, if you knew my true origins—"

Delores was convinced that whatever these two were talking about, they'd go on about it forever. As impolite as it was, she decided she had to interrupt.

"Excuse me?" she said in a loud but friendly voice.

"What?" Kenneth shouted as he turned to look at the newcomers. Valerie stifled a small scream. "What is the meaning of this impropriety?"

"I do apologize for this intrusion," Delores replied smoothly, "but if you gentle people could tell us—"

"We'll do nothing of the sort!" Kenneth retorted. "I've a good mind to thrash the lot of you!"

"Thrashing?" Zabana considered. "Zabana laughs at thrashing."

The Prince of the Jungle's outburst did nothing to calm matters. Kenneth began to tremble. "Cutpurses! Bounders!

I'll show you what it means to break into a lady's home unannounced!" He pulled decisively upon his waistcoat as he started toward Delores and the others. He stumbled before he had taken three steps.

"Kenneth!" Valerie cried in alarm.

"Blast!" He replied before he could recompose himself. "It's nothing. Only my old war injury—"

Valerie gasped. "But you remember what the doctor said—"

"Pray, do not remind me," Kenneth replied bitterly. "It's cruel enough that I shall never be able to play the violin again!"

"We really meant no harm," Delores interjected. "We'd only like to know where we've landed."

But the two in the drawing room didn't even hear her. Valerie placed a delicate hand upon her lace-covered throat. "I'll always love you, wooden finger or no!"

"Maybe we should go out on the street," Louie suggested. "People may be more willing to talk there."

"Valerie!" Kenneth exclaimed.

"How about going to a shaloon?" Doc added. "People alwaysh talk over drinksh!"

"Kenneth!" Valerie replied.

Delores nodded. "Well, we'd better do something, or—"

She had no chance to finish, for the air of the peaceful drawing room was split with fiendish laughter. There was even more blue smoke than before.

Kenneth looked distractedly at the blue fog. "I say, isn't it getting a little close in here?"

"Not as close as its going to get for"—the unmistakable voice of Doctor Dread hesitated triumphantly—"some of you! There is no escape from the minions of Dread! There is no fleeing from"—he paused even more significantly—"your destiny!"

By the time Dread was done pausing, the smoke had cleared, and Delores could see that he had brought Bertha and his other minions along. The minions gave up leering at Delores the moment they recognized her, switching their attentions to Valerie instead.

"See here!" Kenneth objected. "There are certain things not done in polite society!"

"Ah, but we have no time to be"—Dread paused smoothly—"polite. We only have time to be"—he stalled menacingly—"final."

His minions laughed nastily.

"I say," Valerie mentioned, "how did all these people get in here anyway? Has Simpson left the front door open?"

Big Louie sidled up to Delores. He whispered up toward her ear. "But let me tell you about my idea."

Delores frowned down at the sidekick. "You mean we didn't use your idea? I thought you wanted us to use the ring."

"They still aren't cowering!" Big Bertha exclaimed. "How can you have any self-respect as a villain if people don't cower!"

"Cowering?" Zabana scoffed. "Zabana laughs at cowering!"

"Well, yes and no," Louie answered. "But my plan was in the way I wanted to use the ring. That's the trouble with you heroes. It's always act first, think later."

"Perhaps they will cower," Dread suggested with a pause, "—if one or two of them could no longer cower"— he hesitated even more tellingly—"ever again!"

"That's it!" Kenneth exclaimed. "That sounded like a threat to me! I'm going to ring for Simpson and have the lot of you thrown out!"

Delores started to object to Louie's accusation, but she realized he was right. At the first sign of danger, her fists started flying. It was all the fault of Hero School, she supposed; some of those bad habits learned in Jeopardy 101. She remembered how perilous it could get around the dormitories, especially when they were cramming for finals.

"Kenneth!" Valerie whispered passionately. "How forceful!"

Kenneth shrugged manfully. "It is nothing, Valerie. Why, I remember a time during the Boer War—"

"I like it more," Valerie answered, her stiff upper lip beginning to tremble, "when you remind me of the Indian Uprising."

All of Dread's henchpeople cocked their various instruments of death and pointed them at Delores' hardy band.

"I don't think we have time to worry about plans," Delores remarked simply. "Let's blow this joint!" This time, Delores reached over and turned the ring herself. There was the usual blue smoke.

"Oh, Kenneth!" Valerie's voice faded away. "You know if it wasn't for Cyril—"

Delores blinked. She could hardly see anything, even after the smoke cleared. It was night.

Something growled in the darkness. A moment later, that growl was answered by a scream.

"Noises!" came the voice of the jungle prince at her side. "Zabana laughs at noises in the night."

Delores was glad somebody could laugh at this. "Louie," she whispered. "Do you think we should get out of here?"

"It depends," Louie replied frankly. "Where exactly is *here*? This place might be dangerous—"

There was a gurgling, shrieking sound, like somebody drowning in a swamp.

"Then again," Louie continued, "this place might only be very noisy. You take a risk every time you jump from movie world to movie world, especially when that next world is unknown. This particular place might *seem* bad, but where we end up next may be worse. What we're doing now is like playing Russian roulette with a little plastic ring."

Delores tried not to jump when something howled in the distance. That was no way for a hero to act—even if she hadn't quite gotten her diploma. Besides, maybe Louie and Zabana were right. Even though there were all those noises, nothing had happened to them—yet. This world could be quite different when daylight arrived. There was probably no reason for her every sense to be heightened tenfold, her every muscle tensed for action. This place could turn out to be perfectly peaceful, idyllic even—maybe.

There was an odd cry high overhead, half scream, half cackle, like a bird being driven mad in the lightless sky.

"Then again," Louie said, "I could be wrong."

A rumbling came from all too close. It felt as if the ground might be trembling slightly beneath them. Unless, Delores considered, it was the shaking of their collective legs.

"Maybe Zabana have to think twice, too," the jungle prince admitted.

The rumbling grew even closer. Delores looked where she thought the noise was coming from, and realized not all was darkness. There was a light out there. No, it was two lights, two small points of sickly green. They came nearer still, and she noticed a certain oddity about their shapes. They were rounded, almost ovals, like a pair of tiny, glowing fish hanging in the air, or—or disembodied eye sockets glowing from within.

As soon as she had that last thought, she knew it had to be true. The glowing green things were eyes, watching them, coming ever closer. It was hard to judge size or distance in this total absence of light, but those eyes seemed to be growing awfully large.

"Uh-oh," Louie said at her side. So the others could see these glowing orbs as well.

"Eyes? Zabana not afraid of—" The jungle prince stopped abruptly, for he had smelled the same strange stench that had almost made Delores recoil in revulsion; a blast of hot, humid air that carried the putrescent odor of things long dead—vile creatures Delores wouldn't have wanted to meet even when they were alive. There was a sigh of wind, then a growled inhalation.

Whatever was out there had opened its mouth and was breathing on them.

"Maybe we can reashon with it!" Doc suggested from where he had collapsed nearby.

"Maybe we could get out of here!" Louie further suggested.

But Delores knew it was no use. She had seen something in those bright green eyes, something that spoke of finality, and maybe death. The thing had found them now, and in a second, with a single motion of its unseen form, it could decide whether they lived or died.

There was a moment of silence, as deep as the darkness that surrounded them. But the quiet was broken by a single word carried upon the fetid air.

And the word was:

"Slime."

⚊3⚊
"TEENAGE TERROR!"

They say, when you're about to die, that your whole life passes before you.

Roger thought of Gladys, and Andrea, and Phyllis with that funny little smile. Then of course there was Fifi the exchange student, and Nancy with her pom-poms. Those, at least, were all of the girls up to midway through his junior year in high school. After that, of course, it got complicated.

But Roger didn't have time for complications. He was trapped in a car, falling to his doom.

Well, he was chewing gum. At least his ears wouldn't pop. When you worked in public relations, you always tended to look on the bright side.

If only there was some way to save himself, like he and his friends had managed time and again in the Cineverse. If only he had a Captain Crusader Decoder Ring!

But he did have a ring.

Roger felt in his pocket. It was broken, crushed into four pieces by a clumsy foot. But what was broken could be mended. At least it could in theory, if he had the time and the tools. At the very least, there was food for thought.

Well, maybe not food, Roger realized, but there was chewing gum!

He spit the well-chewed gum into his free hand and flattened the wad with his thumb. With this accomplished, he quickly pressed the four broken fragments of the decoder ring into as close an approximation of the original circle as he could manage, being careful to keep the dial free of the makeshift adhesive.

He looked up and out of the car's windshield. The rocks and rolling surf were less than a hundred feet away. It was now or never. Roger closed his eyes and twisted the dial.

"See you in the funny papers!" he shouted.

But where was the blue smoke?

Roger opened his eyes. He was surrounded by bright sun and surf, but he was no longer falling. Oh, he was still strapped into the car, but from what he could see, trapped as he was in his permanent seat belt, all four tires seemed to have sunk in the sand.

Sand? What had happened to the onrushing rocks? And what about the exploding gas tank? Had Roger blacked out for a while? Besides, there was no beach near his mother's house, only sheer cliffs and deadly rocks.

He was someplace different than before. The ring must have worked, at least a little bit. Maybe it had somehow transported him up or down the seacoast, out of harm's way. Roger did his best to study his surroundings from where he was strapped in. Not only was there sand here, but he could hear distant music; electric guitars and something else. Roger strained to hear. Bongos?

Voices and laughter came from behind the car:

"Oh, wow! Groovy!"

"That's a way-out board you've got there, man!"

A pair of blond teenage boys in swimsuits walked up to Roger's window.

"And, Frankie!" said one as he pointed at Roger's jogging suit. "Dig those surfing duds!"

"Hey, Brian!" the other one exclaimed. "Cowabunga! I bet you could really hang ten in those!"

Brian laughed. "What a kook!"

Roger felt a strange disquiet, deep in his stomach. Maybe the ring had really worked after all. He knew one thing for sure: no one talked like this, except in the movies. And he had a terrible feeling what kind of movie this was.

"Hey!" a woman's voice cried out from farther up the beach. "What a crazy woody!"

Now, now, Roger thought, trying to calm himself. Perhaps this was just a serious, dramatic world that was using the beach as but one of its many settings. Roger frowned. Weren't those guitars getting louder?

Brian looked up. "Hey, dig that wild wahini!"

Another woman, also blond, teenage, and—in her case—wearing a psychedelic green bikini, skipped toward them across the sand. Yes, Roger was certain of it now. Those guitars *were* getting louder.

"Hey, Dee Dee!" Frankie called. "Catch our new friend here with the wild wheels!" He looked back in the window at Roger. "Sorry, man. I didn't catch your name."

Roger introduced himself.

"Roger-Dodger!" Brian replied. "This is Dee Dee, the fairest flower on the sand!"

"Tee hee hee," Dee Dee replied as she blushed prettily.

"But hey," Frankie suggested, "we were about to mosey on down the beach to a barbecue. Why don't you come along?"

Roger thanked him, but explained that he was trapped in his seat belt.

"Hey, man," Frankie assured him. "No sweat. We got that covered."

"Yeah!" Dee Dee chirped enthusiastically. "I hear Bix!"

Roger assumed she was referring to the ever louder guitar strums.

"Here they come!" Dee Dee shrieked excitedly.

Roger turned his head as far as he could, trying to see what was making Dee Dee jump up and down in the sand. Four other teens walked out from behind the snack bar, each one carrying a musical instrument. They wore identical shirts, with vertical red and white stripes, and had their hair cut in a "modified-Beatle" style, with bangs just long enough to be blown by the sea wind. The first two carried guitars, the next one a bass. Roger was most impressed with the last fellow, who carried an entire drum kit. He could see the band's name in bright red script on the bass drum: "Bix Bale and the Belltones."

The instruments meant only one thing: Roger's worst fears were realized. This was *that* kind of world.

It took them only a minute to set up their drums and face the ever-growing number of teens that Roger realized now surrounded his car.

"Come on now!" Bix shouted. "Let's shake a tail feather!"

Roger had to face up to it. "This is not just a beach world—" he began aloud, letting the reality sink in.

With that, the band started to play, a full, rich sound despite the fact that Roger could see no wires, microphones or amplifiers.

Roger finished the horrible truth: "—it's a Beach Party Musical world!"

As if in answer, Frankie started to sing:

> "Roger's trapped in his real boss car;
>   Strapped like that, well, he won't get far!
>   It's time to call on Miss Dee Dee;
>   She's a girl who can set him free."

"Hey!" the crowd shouted in unison.

Boom be boom be boom be boom boom boom, the drums replied.

"Nanny nanny-nanny, nanny-nanny hey!" Bix and the Belltones chorused.

This was it, then. Roger was trapped on the most dangerous of all movie worlds, the Musical. He remembered how skeptical he had been when Big Louie had first mentioned the perils of a place like this. But then they had stopped on a movie world where large groups were singing about going to a state fair, and Roger had barely escaped a life judging strawberry jam contests. Then there had been the tropical island, and the song about the Volcano God, which had Roger dancing willingly toward his death!

And wasn't there some place with singing buccaneers? Didn't that have something to do with a man who puffed blue-smoke cigars? But Roger didn't have time to worry about things he couldn't truly remember.

He had witnessed the seductive power of Cineverse music first hand, music which could make you do anything! Music that, unless he fought it with every once of his being, would overtake him again!

Brian sang the second verse:

> "Come on, Dee Dee, now do your stuff.
>   Don't worry, Roger, she won't get rough!
>   She's the answer to all your plans;
>   She's the girl with the magic hands."

"Hey!" the crowd shouted all over again.

Bif de boom de boom bif boom boom, the drums added.

"Nanny nanny-nanny, nanny-nanny hey!" everyone sang together.

Roger looked at Dee Dee. Whatever else the girl had, she sure knew how to dance. She did the frug, the twist, the Watusi and the swim, with some bits of the Phillie and the mashed potato thrown in. Even the psychedelic paisleys on her bikini—which really wasn't very daring as swimsuits went, showing only an inch of tanned flesh between extensive pieces of fabric—even the paisleys seemed to jump about to the thundering surf beat.

And who wouldn't want to dance, with music like this? Twanging guitars, booming drums, and the rhythmic hand-clapping of the crowd made Roger want to move his feet.

"Ow!" he yelled. The seat-belt had dug into Roger's shoulder mid-frug, bringing him back to his senses. He realized that, despite his caution, he was once again falling victim to a musical world. He looked up and saw Dee Dee dancing closer. Brian and Frankie sang a duet:

"So, Roger, now you've met Dee Dee;
    She's the girl who will set you free!
    Here's a little something you won't mind much,
    'Cause she's the girl with the magic touch."

"Hey!" everybody, including Roger, shouted.

Bif boom bang boom bang bif bang bif, the drums announced.

"Nanny nanny-nanny, nanny-nanny hey!" Roger led the chorus.

With that, Dee Dee reached inside the car. Roger's surprise freed him from the music long enough to get a better look at this bikini-clad beauty. She might have been a little younger than the women Roger generally dated, but she did have incredible dimples. If this had been another time and place, and Roger hadn't already met Delores, not to mention all the energy he had to put into saving the Cineverse—

Guitars twanged.

Dee Dee reached for Roger's seat belt.

Drums boomed.

Dee Dee touched the locked metal clasp.

Hands clapped with an urgent rhythm.

The seat belt sprang open!

Dee Dee smiled as she frugged away from the car. Roger

looked down in disbelief at the now-open belt. He was free.

Roger knew what that meant:

Now he could dance!

Roger leapt from the car and started to shing-a-ling. Dee Dee squealed with delight, and began to boogaloo back in his direction. Everybody sang the chorus to that surfing beat:

> "She's the girl with the magic hands,
>   Nanny nanny-nanny, nanny-nanny hey!
>   She's the girl with the magic hands,
>   Nanny nanny-nanny, nanny—"

The chorus was interrupted by the roar of half a dozen motorcycles.

"Oh, what a bring-down!" Brian exclaimed.

"It's the Mad Mumbler and his Motorcycle Mob!" Frankie agreed as he neatly introduced the newcomers.

But the scream of the engines had done more than end the song. They had also brought Roger back to his senses. He realized that Movie Magic had done it to him one more time.

The Cineverse was full of Movie Magic. And it was this very magic—which Big Louie had first explained to Roger when they had both been in the Wild-singing-West—this Movie Magic that could make an arrow fly right through the chain mail and into someone's heart in a Swashbuckler, or could let somebody shoot twelve rounds from a six-shooter in a Western, or could make you forget everything as long as you could dance to the surfing beat in a Beach Party film! Movie Magic was everywhere in the Cineverse, according to Big Louie, eternally helping the plot along!

The bikes roared forward, spewing great clouds of sand in their wake and snapping Roger from his reverie. Everybody around him stepped back to give the biking newcomers room, but Roger wasn't afraid. There was one advantage to being dropped on this world after all. Beach Party movies were always light comedies, with barely enough menace to move the plot along. These motorcycle guys would come up and mouth some ineffectual threats, but everybody knew that if any real problems developed, there would be only one way to resolve them:

The surfing duel!

The six motorcycles rumbled to a halt directly in front of Roger. Two of the cyclists dismounted. Both wore studded motorcycle jackets and heavily patched jeans, but the similarity ended there. One of the gang was almost as big as Zabana, but kept his face hidden behind a large pair of mirrored sun glasses. The other one was a little shorter and so much skinnier that it would have taken three of him to equal the mass of his larger comrade. The smaller man also jerked about now and then for no apparent reason. He paused for a moment to examine the collected surfers, twitched once, then let his mouth split wide in a nasty grin.

"We hear you have a newcomer," he mentioned softly, "so we thought we'd come and introduce ourselves."

"Rssrjjit," the fellow behind him added.

The skinny fellow jerked his head halfway back, then calmly turned his smile to the surfers. "Yeah, right boss. Introduce ourselves. It's only polite. The fellow behind me is the boss. Maybe you've heard of him. They call him the Mad Mumbler."

He hesitated, as if expecting Roger to react in some way to the news of the Mumbler's presence. After a moment's silence, the large fellow mumbled:

"Mzummenya."

"The Mumbler says he's pleased to meet ya," the skinny one translated. "My friends call me Sneer." He jerked violently in Roger's direction. "My enemies don't call me anything. At least not for long."

Roger, figuring that good manners couldn't hurt, said that he was pleased to meet both of them.

"Let's hope you stay that way," Sneer replied. "Seeing that you're a newcomer, there's certain things you gotta understand."

"Really?" Roger replied politely.

"Zrrzsm!" the Mumbler barked.

"Sarcasm!" Sneer translated with a spasm of rage. "The Mad Mumbler knows when he hears sarcasm! And Sneer knows what to do!" He whipped a switchblade from his back pocket.

Switchblade? Roger frowned. The ineffectual gang members in these movies never carried that kind of weapon. It would make them too threatening.

Sneer took a step toward Roger. "Now you listen to the rules. We own this beach. Anybody on the beach does anything, they do it because we say so! Is that clear?"

"Uh," Roger replied, since an answer seemed to be expected here. "Yessir."

"Bskshssh!" the Mumbler screamed.

Sneer moved forward with amazing speed. "Yeah, boss. It sounded like back talk to me, too!"

Somehow, Sneer's left hand had grabbed Roger's jogging suit, and the knife was pressed against the tip of Roger's nose.

"The Motorcycle Mob runs everything around here!" Sneer shouted in Roger's face. "And we will until somebody rides the Cowabunga-munga!"

Roger couldn't help himself. "The Cowabunga-munga?"

"Trrmrssrssr," the mumbler rumbled.

"Yeah," Sneer agreed. "Once a troublemaker, always a troublemaker. Everybody knows the Cowabunga-munga—"

"Yeah!" all the surrounding surfers and beach bunnies interjected.

"—that sensation of the surf that makes a tidal wave look like a small potato. It's the monster mother of the sea, and it only comes to our beach once every seven years!" He looked out at the ocean, twitching respectfully. "And the guy who rides it *rules* the beach!"

This was more like it, Roger thought. He had started to worry, with that knife in his nose, that maybe the Change had caused some alterations in this beach party planet, making it a lot more dangerous than those innocuous movies Roger remembered. But knife or no knife, what this guy was doing now was challenging him to a surfing duel. So maybe things hadn't changed that much after all.

Roger knew what was expected of him. He asked: "The Cowabunga-munga? When's it going to come again?"

"As if you didn't know!" Sneer drove the hilt of his switchblade into Roger's stomach. Roger staggered back into Dee Dee. That hurt! Things weren't supposed to hurt in Beach Party movies.

It had to be the Change—changing even a world as innocuous as this. Roger realized this place might really be dangerous. Maybe he'd have to use his ring sooner than he'd expected.

But, Roger further realized, if the Change was still doing this kind of damage, there might not be a single safe place in all of the Cineverse.

"Crssrrss," the Mumbler interjected.

"Yeah, boss," Sneer replied. "He is a pretty cool character. I wonder how cool he'd be if I cut his lady, instead!"

The knife hilt stroked Dee Dee's side.

"Tee hee hee," Dee Dee replied.

"Laugh at me!" Sneer shrieked. "She laughed at me!"

"It tickled!" Dee Dee protested.

"Trsrfmmbm!" the Mumbler stated.

Sneer's smile grew even more deformed. "Yeah, boss, they're both troublemakers!" His knife followed the line of Roger's shoulder. "And you know what we do with troublemakers!"

Dee Dee shrieked and grabbed Roger from behind, binding his arms to his sides. She had a very powerful grip for a beach bunny. Roger couldn't free his hands to reach into his pocket to get the ring.

The Mad Mumbler laughed. Sneer giggled. The background motorcycle gang guffawed. The knife returned to Roger's nose.

Roger realized that he couldn't use the ring in any case; not if it meant leaving Dee Dee behind to face these thugs. That sort of thing would be against everything Captain Crusader had ever stood for. No matter what the Change had done to the Cineverse, Roger realized, it still wouldn't be the heroic thing to do.

The Mad Mumbler pointed a trembling finger at Roger. "Krrit!"

"Cut him?" Sneer laughed. "Yeah, boss. *Where* should I cut him?"

Cut? Were they serious? Roger decided he needed to re-revise his plans. Maybe he could use the ring and take Dee Dee with him. If he could only somehow free his arms!

"Hahrrr," the Mumbler insisted.

"There?" Sneer sneered. "That's a serious cut, boss. It just shows what can happen if you use sarcasm." He winked at Roger. "Say your prayers, ho-daddy!"

Sneer lunged forward, his knife aimed straight for Roger's chest!

4

"The Dog Means Death!"

"Slime?" Big Louie replied.

"Slime!" the monstrous voice reiterated. "Slime is my life!"

Delores didn't like this.

"This wasn't my idea," Big Louie reminded her.

Maybe it was time to use the decoder ring. Wherever they ended up had to be better than this. But Delores knew they had to be cautious. What had Louie said; something about Russian roulette with a plastic ring? It would be easy to make a mistake in the total darkness, especially when facing something as potentially supernatural as whatever now breathed on them from out in the murk. What was it? What could it do? She wanted to be very careful they didn't use the ring to go somewhere else, only to somehow bring the slime creature along.

"You," the voice commanded.

"Who?" Delores asked with some trepidation.

"Not me," Louie put in all too hastily. "I hope."

35

"Not any of us!" Zabana suggested boldly. "Thing has us confused with four other people!"

"Let'sh jusht invite it for a drink!" Doc suggested from somewhere around ground level.

"The woman," the voice explained.

Delores tried to laugh. "Uh, guys? Perhaps it *is* time for a change of scene."

"It is no use," the voice replied. "There is no escape. Slime is your destiny."

There was an explosion, followed by the all-too-familiar oily laughter. Delores was sure, had there been any light, they would have all been surrounded by blue smoke. The archest of archvillains had found them again.

"It is no use!" Dread chortled. "There is no escape!"

"You're stealing my lines," a monstrous voice interjected.

"Pitiful fools," Dread continued, "don't you realize I have made certain adjustments to my ring that will allow me to follow you any—" He paused. "Eh? Did somebody say something?"

"There is only one response to line thieves," the voice replied. "Slime."

"Come now, Delores," Dread chided. "How childish! Trying to confuse me by—disguising your voice? You can't fool me that easily. What do you take me—*ick*—what is this stuff—where is it coming—*blechh*—get it off me—*ugh*—I can hardly move. It's already up—*glub*—around my—*gurgle*."

Doctor Dread was heard no more.

"Out of here?" Louie whispered.

"Out of here!" Delores agreed. "Grab hold, fellas!" She felt Louie's hand on her arm, and Zabana's on her shoulder. A moment later, Doc grabbed her ankle.

"Up, up, and away!" Delores announced as she twisted the ring.

There was the usual explosion, and they were gone. On

the whole, however, Delores would have felt better if she had not heard those last few words:

"There is no escape from slime."

"This is more like it!" Louie announced happily.

It was night, and the world was devoid of color. This didn't seem very promising, either, except that Louie liked it for some reason. Delores only hoped it was better than that dreadful place they had just escaped. There was light here, after all, even though it was a harsh, white light that threw long, dark shadows across the alleyway. And the shadows looked like nothing so much as bars on a cage. Far away, Delores could hear a woman's laughter, the plaintive call of a saxophone, and the wail of police sirens.

"This is the city," Louie explained. "This is where I belong. This is a place where a guy in a double-breasted suit can feel comfortable." He looked down at the cowboy duds he still wore. "Now if only I had my double-breasted suit back, we'd be fine." He shrugged apologetically as he began a furtive walk to the street at the alley's end. "Otherwise," he called softly over his shoulder, "we might have some trouble."

This time, Delores understood what Louie was talking about. Since they were dressed as two cowboys, a jungle prince, and a woman who was about to be sacrificed to a volcano god, they might not blend in here. But this was Louie's home world. There must be some way to find less conspicuous clothing, and she was sure the sidekick could help them there. With luck, maybe she could get out of this stupid muumuu and back into something more comfortable, like a black vinyl jumpsuit.

She walked after Louie, waving for Doc and Zabana to follow. Once they blended a little more fully into their surroundings, it would be time to think about other things. This was the sort of decision she had learned in Heroic Strategy 201; if this was a place that Louie truly knew, maybe it was time to stop running, and make plans.

Delores felt a slight shiver roll across her spine and shoulders, a reaction, no doubt, to the terrors of that dark world they had just left. Still, they had escaped the place cleanly, as Dread faced the wrath of the thing that had first threatened them.

Whatever they had met in the darkness had—at the very least—inconvenienced Dread. Delores was all too aware of the resources of their nemesis to believe that he had been eliminated. But he had been delayed. That would have to be enough. It proved heroes could still beat the odds on occasion, even after the Change.

Louie reached the end of the alleyway. He took off his ten-gallon hat and peered around the corner.

Delores crept up behind him. "What should we do?" she whispered.

"How should I know?" he whispered back. "I'm only a sidekick."

"I'll find a shaloon," Doc ventured from where he crawled behind them.

"Zabana lead way!" the big fellow offered. "Laugh at all who stand before us. Beat, strangle, stab with hunting knife! Zabana not only Prince of Jungle. He prince of everywhere!"

"Uh, no," Delores replied immediately. "I'll lead the way. Unless—" She stopped herself, her heroic instincts temporarily overcome by pragmatism. "Louie, do you know of any used-clothing stores around here?"

Louie grinned at that, glad at last to be given a sidekick sort of thing to do. He led them as quickly as possible down the deserted streets to a place called Second Avenue Second Hand. Strangely enough, even though it appeared to be the middle of the night, the store was open for business. Delores thought she heard gunshots as she opened the store's front door, but they were behind her, somewhere in the distance, as were the shouts, screams, and sirens that followed. She quickly ushered the others inside.

A little bell rang as the door shut behind them, closing

out the noise from the street. Delores glanced around the shop. It was awfully spacious in here, much larger than it appeared from the street; more of a warehouse than a storefront. Bright electric bulbs were hung along the ceiling, but half their light was lost in the dust that surrounded the shelves and tables piled high with clothes. The light bulbs seemed to stretch away as far as Delores could see, but half this place was still lost in shadow.

"It's awfully quiet," Delores whispered.

"Like a tomb," Louie agreed.

"It looks deserted," Delores observed. "I wonder if anyone's here?"

"May I help you?"

The words were spoken in a conversational, if efficient, tone. After all the whispering, it sounded to Delores as if someone had shouted in her ear.

A small, bent man stood directly before them in a narrow aisle between the mounds. He had probably only stepped out of the heavy shadows, but it seemed as if he had appeared out of nowhere. He smiled at his customers.

Delores exhaled. There was nothing to be upset about. She was glad she'd only jumped a little bit, and hadn't yelled at all.

"We need some new outfits," Louie explained.

"That I can see." The small man nodded pleasantly, as if having two cowboys, a jungle prince, and a woman in a muumuu walk into your store was an everyday occurrence. He waved at the piles of clothing on either side. "This is the place."

Delores and the others got to work. Louie found a double-breasted suit for himself, and another one for Doc. They had some problems with Zabana, but after certain alterations were made on the better part of a pair of double-breasted suits—which were thereupon sewn together—he too looked as if he belonged on this world.

They were interrupted once.

The door slammed open. A man took a step inside, but

stood strangely erect as machine gun fire erupted outside. The man staggered forward one step, then back two, before falling on the sidewalk outside.

The door slammed closed.

"Happens all the time," the proprietor confessed with a shrug. "Think nothing of it. It's the neighborhood."

Delores continued her search. She wasn't having as much luck as the others. Apparently, black vinyl jumpsuits were not in fashion on this world, and she had to settle for a simple, spangled evening dress. Her only consolation was that the garment had padded shoulders.

There was, of course, a little problem when Delores and her fellows realized they had no money to pay for all these goods. However, once the proprietor was informed that they were all heroes (and Zabana was a very *big* hero) they had no further problem. Heroes always paid—eventually.

Delores just hoped the villains would pay first.

Speaking of villains, she wouldn't want to be caught after she and her fellows had made all these preparations. They had already spent a bit longer choosing their wardrobes than she might have liked. She looked out and frowned at the night sky. "We'd better get out of here before daylight."

"Daylight?" the proprietor replied. "It's hardly ever daylight around here."

The storekeeper smiled enigmatically as he disappeared in the shadows.

They were alone again, facing the door outside.

"Where now?" she asked Big Louie.

"I've got to pick again?" the sidekick complained.

Delores nodded. "We need someplace safe, where we can make our plans."

"Safe?" Louie asked incredulously. "In a *Film Noir* world? You've got to be kidding."

Delores saw Louie's point. If a secondhand clothing emporium could be this sinister, imagine what the rest of this world held in store.

"Well, if not safe," she asked instead, "how about out of the way?"

"Out of the way?" This time he smiled. "Louie's a specialist in out of the way. It comes with being a sidekick. Let's see—my uncle owns a gin joint; a little hole in the wall."

"That shounds more like it!" Doc enthused.

This time, even Delores had to agree.

Joe's Place. At three or four A.M.—whatever time it was—the bar was almost deserted. Delores nevertheless picked a corner table for the four of them to huddle around. It kept them out of the way, discouraged eavesdropping, made them less of a target. In a place like this, you had to take every precaution.

Louie's uncle hadn't arrived yet. The bartender said he came on in a couple hours—at six—when the joint really started to jump. Louie said that was just as well. It was probably better if they didn't meet any of his family. Delores didn't find that last remark particularly reassuring.

It was dark in here. Almost as dark as—but no, Delores had told herself she wasn't going to dwell on that other place. They had more important things to do, like saving the Cineverse! She could barely see her companions' faces in the dim and smoky light.

On the jukebox, a woman sang about the man who got away.

Doc had a drink.

"So what do we do?" she asked.

"Zabana say we save Roger," the jungle prince offered.

Louie sighed. "There's a problem there. When Roger lost the ring, mid-transit, he—"

"Went back to home world!" Zabana interjected impatiently. "Even Prince of Jungle knows that!"

"Yeah," Louie agreed. "But there's something that I know and you don't. Remember, I used to be a member of Doctor Dread's gang." He hesitated, staring down at the table. "I know what was waiting for Roger back on his home world."

"You mean Dread set a trap?" Delores asked.

Louie nodded unhappily. "The nefarious Doctor thought of everything, including having one of his henchpeople waiting for Roger back on Earth. And not just any henchperson, either. The fellow waiting for Roger was"—Louie paused to take a ragged breath—"Menge the Merciless."

Delores gasped.

Zabana flexed his jungle-bred muscles.

"Roger not have chance!"

Doc had a drink.

Delores couldn't believe it. Not Roger. Not a man who knew movies the way most men knew their receding hairlines. She shook her head.

"I won't know that Roger's dead until I see it for myself. There's something different about that man. Maybe he's really a hero—" She stopped herself. Perhaps that was going too far. Instead, she added, "—or maybe he's something else altogether."

"But Menge the Merciless!" Louie insisted.

Delores knew, realistically, that Louie was right. Menge would have killed Roger instantly. Unless Roger had somehow managed to escape. There were so many escapes for a man who knew movies like that! And there was something in her that simply refused to think of Roger dead.

Maybe it was her emotions talking, rather than her intellect. But Delores knew, if Roger was still alive, he probably was somewhere in the Cineverse. And there was only one person, besides Roger himself, who would definitely know his whereabouts, who indeed knew all there was to know about the Cineverse.

"Very well," Delores said grimly. "Then we must find Captain Crusader!"

Doc pushed the bottle out of the way.

"That's serious business, missy."

Delores frowned. There was something different about Doc's voice.

"What do you mean?" she asked.

Doc smiled wryly. "How do you find somebody who doesn't want to be found?"

Yes! Delores was certain of it now. Not only was Doc's slur gone, but his voice had become more forceful—even heroic.

"What do you mean?" Louie asked. "We've already seen Captain Crusader!"

"In three different disguises," Doc reminded the sidekick, "as a masked marshal, a tribal chieftain, and a mysterious island drummer. And, every time we're about to discover his true identity, he spouts one of those sayin's of his. You know—'The Dewey Decimal System is your friend!' or some such—and then he ups and disappears. Does that sound to you like a fella who wants to be found?"

"I never thought of it like that," Louie admitted.

Delores nodded in admiration of Doc's reasoning. "That means there's more than one secret out there. Not only are we unaware of the fine points of Doctor Dread's plan to conquer the Cineverse, we don't even know the true direction of Captain Crusader's counterplan."

"If he even has one," Doc added gently.

"But, that's almost unthinkable!" Delores objected. "He's Captain Crusader! He must have a plan!"

"I'm sure he had one, once," Doc replied, still not raising his voice. "But the Change did more than bring unhappy endings to the Cineverse. Think of what it's done to us, and to all those around us. What if the alterations that have occurred in the very fabric of the Cineverse have affected its ultimate hero?"

"You mean," Louie said in horror, "what if the Change changed Captain Crusader?"

"It's certainly possible," Doc agreed. "It's just a little somethin' I studied when I held the Wild Bill Hickok Philosophy Chair at Western States University. That was, of course, before I became the Tombstone town drunk." He stared moodily at the bottle before him. "But I brought it up to make a point. With things the way they are now, we can't take nothin' for granted."

"You've changed, Doc," Delores mentioned.

The cowpoke pushed the bottle away. "All things in moderation." He looked back up at Delores. "When I first met Roger, he inspired me. He wasn't content to just let the plot go by. He wanted to change things, for the better! He reminded me of my heroin' days, before the bottle got the better of me. I swore I'd lay off the sauce, and for a while, the action and adventurin' saw me through. But playing the town drunk in a thousand Western plots has taken its toll. I can be a hero, still, but I gotta be a little drunk, first. And I can get drunk on almost anythin'."

"So that's why your slur's gone!" Delores exclaimed.

"Yes, it is, little missy," Doc modestly agreed. "Simply said, I shall certainly sustain a successful level of sobriety. She sells sea shells down by the sea sho—"

The doors to the gin joint slammed open. Slamming doors, machine-gun fire, people staggering out of clothing stores in the night—Delores reminded herself that all this was nothing to worry about. Still, any hopes that the gin joint might be in the same sort of neighborhood as Second Avenue Second Hand evaporated when Delores heard the diabolical laughter.

"How—convenient!" Dread's oily voice shouted over the sound of countless minions filing into the bar. "That we should find the very ones we seek, hiding in a bar owned by"—he hesitated triumphantly—"Bertha's uncle!"

"Oh, yeah," Louie said in a small voice, "did I tell you that Dread's number-one-henchperson was also my sister?"

"Lucky for us," Doc chuckled, "this here suit has large enough pockets for my six-shooters."

The jungle prince stood abruptly, almost tipping over the table. "Zabana say we save Cineverse!"

Delores cursed her foolishness as she stood, too, her back to the wall. She had forgotten about Louie's sister. And the fact that this wasn't only Louie's home planet, but was Dread's base of operations as well.

The henchmen continued to file in, row on row of slouch hats and double-breasted pin stripes. Delores had never seen so many minions! What other mistakes had she made? She had let her concern for Roger and the Cineverse get in the way of her own self-preservation. Now, she might not only have sealed her own fate, but the fates of the three men who had trusted her.

The door slammed behind the last of Dread's lackeys. But there must have been close to a hundred of them, all crammed into this tiny neighborhood bar, all smiling evilly beneath their broad-brimmed hats as they lifted their gats and roscoes to finish off the four heroes standing in the corner. And in the center of them all was Doctor Dread, his green snakesuit costume gleaming malevolently even in the bar's dim light, and Big Bertha, who was wearing something that looked an awful lot like a black vinyl jumpsuit!

"De—lor—es," Doctor Dread jeered, speaking so slowly that every syllable was like a separate word. "How—pleasant—for us. How—unpleasant—for you."

But Delores refused to be shaken by the evildoer's taunts. Somehow she'd best this beast with his hundred helpers! And even more than that, she wouldn't be shot by a woman in a costume that—by all rights of heroic priority—should be hers! There must be some way out of this! She had to find one, for the sake of Roger, and the Cineverse!

"But I am not without my—mercy," Dread allowed. "Tell me, De—lor—es, do I hear any last—groveling—pleas to spare your—worthless—lives?"

For her answer, Delores spat on his polished snakeskin shoes.

"Very well." The King of Crime looked meaningfully

at his room full of minions. "You know what to do, men."
Dread hesitated tellingly. "Discard them!"

"Hey, boss!" someone shouted. "Who let in this dog?"

Dog? Delores thought.

That's when all the guns went off.

⟁ 5 ⟁

"Atomic Disaster!"

"Mrrssrrss!"

Roger was pushed roughly to the ground. He looked up, and saw the great bulk of the Mad Mumbler standing between him and Sneer's knife. The gang leader had somehow moved even faster than his lackey, saving Roger from a blade in his chest!

"Jsss Crsssssss!" the Mumbler yelled down at the trembling Sneer. "Mnnff Mffnn!"

"Yeah, boss?" Sneer stared down at his switchblade, somewhat shaken. "What was that?"

"Wsskssoiss mffnnifnn!" the Mumbler insisted.

Sneer stared back at his boss. "You *didn't* say to cut him?"

The gang leader made a slashing motion with his hand. "Mssxxmm vbbllmm!"

"Oh! You said for *me* to cut it out!"

"Wccsblffmm znrrgssbll!"

"Oh, is *that* what you meant?" Sneer shrugged. "Well, I can't help it if you won't speak up!"

"Jrsdlpplll!" The Mumbler pushed Sneer back into the sand with a flick of his hand. Roger found himself grabbed by the gang leader's free hand, which was the approximate size of an uncanned ham, and hoisted back to his feet.

Sneer picked himself up and brushed himself off, muttering something about people who mumbled idioms under their breaths.

"Srrbbbttt," the leader mumbled in Roger's direction.

Roger made an expression that he hoped was a friendly smile. "Don't worry. No harm done."

"Srrzzssmm!" the Mumbler screamed.

Oh, no, Roger thought. Not this again.

"No, I am not being sarcastic!" Roger yelled back. "Don't you know when somebody's trying to be friendly?"

Roger felt a hand on either shoulder. He looked back, and saw Frankie on one side, Brian on the other.

"I don't know how to put this to you, but—" Frankie began.

"Nobody's ever friendly with the Motorcycle Mob—" Brian continued.

Frankie added: "It just isn't done—"

Brian explained: "It's one of the Rules of the Beach—"

"Yeah!" Frankie exclaimed. "Right up there with 'Shoes and shirts must be worn at all times when in this—' "

"Well, I'm changing the rules here and now!" Roger admitted it; he was sick and tired of the rigamarole he encountered every time he landed on a new movie world. That was one of the hidden dangers of the Cineverse—one wrong move, and you could be caught up in some local plot for hours, even days. He had spent far too long in this place already. He had certainly blown any chance of rescuing anybody. Delores might be dead right now, or in the hands of that archfiend, Doctor Dread. And what was Roger doing? Having a conversation with a bunch of beach-blanket bozos!

Or at least he was until he had made that declaration. Now, there was not a sound around him except for the surf breaking on the sand. Everyone—surfers, beach bunnies, the Motorcycle Mob, Bix Bale and the Belltones—they were all staring at him, and, of the entire incredibly tanned group, only Dee Dee looked the least bit friendly.

"Oops," Roger said aloud. Perhaps, by speaking his mind, he had broken an even bigger rule.

"Tee hee hee," Dee Dee giggled sympathetically.

The Mad Mumbler's voice broke the silence: "Bssfzzll!"

Sneer's smile once again stretched across his lips. "Yeah, big boss man. Maybe we *were* too easy on him." He stroked the handle of his switchblade.

Roger could see it happening all over again. This corner of the Cineverse wanted to force him back into a role. He felt the anger growing inside him once again.

"Oh, no!" he declared. "I'm not going through this again!"

The Mumbler made a strangling motion with his hands. "Thrssnnddll!"

"Yeah, boss, threats don't worry him, do they?" Sneer twirled his knife toward the surrounding surfers. "Maybe we should cut up his friends, too."

All the surfers took a step away. All except one.

Dee Dee still giggled at Roger's side.

Roger realized he'd done it now. It was time to make his stand. But he had to use his anger in the right sort of way— a way that would work for him in the Cineverse. If he was going to be forced into a role, it would be a role of his own choosing. He wished he had a toothpick to chew on, or a pack of Luckies he could roll up inside the sleeve of his T-shirt—that is, if he had a T-shirt. But he didn't have time to find props; he'd have to do it on style alone. He planted both feet firmly in the sand and stared at the members of the Motorcycle Mob.

"Nah, you can't change my mind with threats. I'm not just gonna change the rules—" He paused dramatically. "I'm gonna make up my own—"

Everyone around him gasped as a group. It clearly was

the sort of thing that Was Not Done on a beach party planet. But Roger knew there was no backing down, especially where there was a motorcycle gang around. Especially a motorcycle gang that had now all drawn their switchblades.

Maybe, Roger considered, he had gone too far.

The other motorcycle members smiled to match Sneer.

It wouldn't do him any good to be this angry, if he was also dead.

Many of their smiles were missing many of their teeth.

But he had gotten out of situations worse than this in the Cineverse.

The gang members picked at their teeth with their knives.

Once again, Roger told himself to think like a movie.

My, they certainly were nice, long, sharp knives.

He swallowed, then finished his sentence.

"—even if it takes riding the Cowabunga-munga to do it!"

And everyone took another step away. Their collective gasp this time held a hint of awe. The knife-wielders paused in their teeth picking, their blades ready to cut through the tension-filled air at any second.

They all knew Roger was proposing a surfing duel.

"That's pretty big talk—" Frankie ventured.

"We've never even seen you surf—" Brian mentioned.

"Yeah, man! Where's your board—" Frankie added.

"And, like, the big wave isn't even coming until tomorrow!" Brian concluded.

"Sounds like some kind of ho-daddy excuse to me!" Sneer brandished his blade. "I say we cut him anyway!"

"Gllffgrrggll!" the Mumbler agreed.

The other gang members all started talking at once.

"Yeah, blood!"

They laughed nastily.

"The girl, too!"

They chuckled disagreeably.

"—carve some initials—"

They guffawed coarsely.

"—real deep tattoos!"

They hooted malevolently.

Roger had had enough of this.

"Dee Dee!" he shouted.

"Tee hee hee!" Dee Dee replied.

"Grab my hand!" Roger instructed.

"Tee hee hee!" was Dee Dee's response.

"Hey, Roger-Dodger," Brian said, "you don't have to worry about these guys."

"That's right!" Frankie added. "Those guys won't be able to do a thing once we start another song!"

"No!" Roger shouted all too vehemently. He might be able to survive a knife cut or two. But Roger knew, if Bix Bale and the Belltones should do so much as twang a guitar string, he would be sucked into this surfing world forever.

He reached into his pocket with his free hand and pulled out the chewing-gum-encased ring. But how could he turn it without letting go of Dee Dee?

"Oh, yeah?" Sneer vituperated. "None of you can stop us!"

The entire Motorcycle Mob took a collectively threatening step toward Roger and Dee Dee.

Roger pushed the gummed ring against his ring finger. Now, if he could only push the dial around a bit with his thumb. Roger bit his lower lip. His thumb jerked against the ring, almost knocking it from his hand. He managed to close his fist about the ring before it fell, his heart leaping about in his chest. He would have to be much more careful. Especially with the ring broken the way it was, there was no safe way to turn it without using both hands.

"Frrnnnstbblll!" the Mumbler pointed out.

Sneer agreed. "He's got something in his hand. It looks like he's going to try some funny stuff!"

Then again, Roger realized that he didn't have to hold Dee Dee for both of them to escape. All that was necessary was for Dee Dee to have a hold on him.

"Dee Dee!" he instructed. "Put your hand around my waist!"

The beach bunny giggled girlishly.

"Ccrrkkvvbbmmnnzzwwll!" the Mumbler urged as he drew a ragged breath.

"See?" Sneer elucidated. "He's going to try some surfer trick!"

"Roger Dodger!" Brian called anxiously. "Are you *sure* you wouldn't like to hear another song?"

Dee Dee let go of Roger's hand and put her arm around his waist. She stepped close to hug him tight. Roger reached around her as well. Now, if he could just get his free hand on the ring. . . .

"Mssgllcklllpssfnnrrwttghjjjssk!" the Mumbler screamed, turning a very nice shade of blue in the process.

Dee Dee giggled in his ear. Roger admitted it: Even in a tense situation like this, it was distracting to hold a bikini-clad woman in your arms when you were trying to use your Captain Crusader Decoder Ring.

"Okay, boss!" Sneer announced with a jerk of his head. "Full frontal attack!"

That's when the ring slipped out of Roger's fingers.

"Tee hee hee," Dee Dee remarked as she deftly caught it.

"Snnrrk!" The Mumbler managed between great, gasping breaths. "Snnrrk!"

"Cut them now!" Sneer instructed as the mob ran at them through the sand.

What, Roger despaired, could they do? A half dozen leather-jacketed mobsters were bearing down on them as fast as they could make their way through the sand. Their very sharp knives glittered in the seaside sun.

"See you in the funny papers!" Roger yelled despite everything.

"Tee hee hee," Dee Dee replied nervously.

The sand was covered with blue smoke.

• • •

The smoke cleared. Roger and Dee Dee stood on a suburban street.

"Tee hee—" Dee Dee began nervously. "tee—" She took a ragged breath. "Oh, thank the Cineverse! I'm no longer there!"

"Pardon?" Roger replied.

Dee Dee gave Roger's arm a comradely pat as she disengaged herself. "The Beach Party world! You've helped me escape. I can't thank you enough. Oh, but we haven't been properly introduced. Dr. Dee Dee Davenport, at your service." She shook Roger's hand heartily.

Roger thought to close his mouth. Somehow, this woman seemed almost completely different from the beach beauty he'd so recently hugged on the surfing world.

Dr. Davenport glanced down at her psychedelic green bikini. "Oh, but this is so . . . so . . . *inappropriate*!" She frowned in a determined sort of way. "It's lucky we materialized right around the corner from the Institute."

She walked forward, her strides long and purposeful. Roger had to run to catch up.

Roger couldn't help but marvel how different this place was from all the other movie worlds he had found himself on. He looked up and down the street at two rows of white tract houses set back from the street by an acre or so of manicured green lawns. Not that there was anything particularly special about this place. But that was it exactly. His surroundings were just so incredibly undistinguished. It could have been almost Anywhere, U.S.A. That's exactly what made it so strange.

Any doubts that he was still in the Cineverse were instantly dispelled when he read the street sign on the corner. One sign read "Anywhere Terrace," the other "Hometown Lane." He had fallen into what looked like the ultimate, mid-American movie world. But what happened on mid-American movie worlds? Roger had this sudden vision of domestic comedies about the trials of raising sixteen children. He shivered.

"Here we are!" Dr. Davenport led him up the driveway of a brick building a bit larger than those around the corner. A large bronze plaque by the door announced that this was "The Southern California Institute of Very Advanced Science."

So this must be the institute that Dee Dee—or Dr. Davenport, Roger corrected himself—so recently referred to. Roger admitted it. Once again, he was thoroughly confused. This had become a nagging problem ever since he had first found himself in the Cineverse: How could he ever hope to save anybody if he could never figure out what was going on?

Dr. Davenport opened the front door. Roger followed her inside. She pulled a pair of long white lab coats off a rack against one wall and handed one to Roger. She quickly put the other one on.

She smiled. "At last! I feel dressed again!"

Roger noticed that the coat had a badge pinned to its plastic pocket pen protector; a badge that read DR. DAVENPORT.

"Here," the doctor instructed, "put yours on, too. Trust me. It gives you credibility."

Roger shrugged the coat over his shoulders. The badge on his pocket protector read GUEST.

"Come on now," she said as she once again boldly strode ahead. "It's time to get to work." She opened a second door, covered by a sign that read RESTRICTED AREA! AUTHORIZED PERSONNEL ONLY!

A security guard looked up as they entered. "Dr. Davenport! Thank goodness you're here!"

"Yes, Smedley," she replied. "It feels good to be back."

"No," Smedley answered vehemently. "You don't understand. It's much worse than that. It's the Nucleotron!"

Dee Dee gasped. "The Nucleotron? But that means—"

Smedley nodded, confirming her worst fears. "The slime monster is gone!"

A red light began to blink above Smedley's desk. Somewhere in the distance Roger could hear the wail of sirens.

"It's nearing critical mass!" Dr. Davenport ran down the hall. "Quick, Roger! If we don't do something soon, it's going to blow us all to Kingdom Come!"

⌐ **6** ⌐
"Dread Destination!"

"Bark bark! Yip yip arf!"

The dog's barking somehow rose over the gunfire.

"Yip bark! Arf yip bark!"

The shooting stopped.

Delores wondered if she should risk a look. She and her fellows had all taken refuge behind the large oak table that Zabana, with his jungle-bred reflexes, had tipped to one side in the same instant that the first shot was fired. So far, the wood had taken the brunt of the assault, and Doc had pulled his six-shooters from his deep suitcoat pockets, ready to pay back the villains in kind.

"You'll"—Doctor Dread's voice hesitated menacingly—"suffer for this!"

Doc peeked around the table's edge, guns at the ready.

"Well, I'll be doggone!" he exclaimed instead.

"Bark yip! Bark yip growl!" the dog replied.

Doc grinned down at his allies. "You all should take a look at this. It's plumb amusin'."

Delores cautiously peered out from behind the barricade,

ever alert for treachery. Her mouth fell open. She had never expected this.

Everyone, all hundred of Dread's lackeys, seemed frozen in place. And all of them watched the drama unfolding at the very center of the room. There, flat on his back, was Doctor Dread, with a white German shepherd standing on his chest.

"Yip yip bark!" the dog remarked, its voice somewhat muffled since its teeth had already pierced the material on Dread's snakeskin cowl—the same teeth that were now a fraction of an inch from the villain's neck!

"This is your last chance!" Dread declared one last time. "Before you are"—his hesitation sounded more uncertain than usual—"subtracted!"

The German shepherd only growled in response. Delores frowned. Where had she seen that dog before?

"All right, now!" a voice called in merrily through the now open door. "What's all the ruckus?"

"Yip yip!" the dog replied. "Bark bark yip!"

"Why," said the voice from the door, "it almost sounds like the little fella's talkin'." A rotund, white-haired police officer with a twinkle in his eye stepped into the bar.

"Officer O'Clanrahan!" Big Louie shouted.

"The very same, boyo," the policeman acknowledged, broadly winking at one and all. "And I've brought my special helper along, too."

The shepherd wagged his tail as the policeman approached.

"That Dwight the Wonder Dog!" Zabana exclaimed in astonishment.

"Right you are, big fella," O'Clanrahan agreed. "Everybody knows Dwight the Wonder Dog."

They did? Delores frowned again. Then why didn't she? Maybe she had been spending too much time in Hero School. Still, even she had thought the dog looked familiar.

"Yip bark arf!" Dwight agreed as O'Clanrahan leaned down to scratch him behind the ears.

But the shepherd had relaxed his vigilance. It was only for a fraction of a second, but it was a fraction too much. Dread shifted and rolled, and Dwight lost his footing. The dog had to scamper back half a dozen feet as Dread scrambled to his feet, and Officer O'Clanrahan found himself staring into the business end of Big Bertha's roscoe.

"Faith and begorrah!" the policeman whispered.

"Yip yip arf!" Dwight barked apologetically. "Yip yip yip!"

"Yeah, boy," Louie replied. "It just might work."

Doctor Dread laughed, a sound to chill both flesh and bone. "Things seem to have—changed, don't they?" He glanced around at his hundred mobsters. "Now, who do you suppose we should—erase first?"

The dog and Officer O'Clanrahan neatly split the largest number of votes. But Big Bertha had other ideas.

"Kill her." She waved her gat at Delores. "She's the ringleader. Without her, the others are lost."

"Such language!" Dread reprimanded. "Still, there is a certain—logic in proposing Delores'—removal."

That's when Big Louie screamed.

Dwight jumped up onto his hind legs.

"He's walking backwards!" one of the gang members observed as the dog approached the leering Dread.

The shepherd whined suddenly and flopped to the ground.

"He's rolling over," another gangster commented.

"Fools!" Dread began. "Don't you—"

But, before the villain could even hesitate meaningfully, Dwight had rolled over on his back, all four paws in the air and head to one side.

"He's playing dead!" one of the evil band exclaimed.

"Oh, how lifelike!" another enthused.

"—realize," Dread continued, "this is but a clever—" He paused tellingly.

"Now!" Louie shouted.

Dwight's still snout suddenly snapped around the arch-fiend's leg. Uttering a cry equally divided between surprise and pain, Dread once again toppled to the ground.

Doc shot the roscoe from Big Bertha's hand, then trained both his six-shooters on the horizontal mastermind.

Dread's groan held a particularly sinister edge. He slowly turned his head to stare malevolently at Delores and her cohorts. His words were even slower and more fraught with meaning than usual:

"You don't expect to escape—unavenged."

There was a moment of uncomfortable silence. It was true, Delores thought. They had won the battle. But what good would it do them if they could never get out of Joe's Bar?

"Yip, yip! Bark bark bark!" Dwight announced.

"Of course not," Louie added as he smiled at Dread. "The Doctor won't be able to avenge anything. Dread is coming with us."

The bad guys snarled collectively.

"Try anything," Doc drawled, "and I'll show you why I won two blue ribbons at the Wild West Territorial Fair."

"Two blue ribbons?" Big Bertha's voice held a grudging respect.

"Well, only one of them was for shootin'," Doc admitted. "More than that would have been redundant. Got the other one for cannin'."

"Canning?" Big Louie asked.

Doc nodded. "Best dandelion preserves northwest of the Pecos."

"What if I"—Dread paused with great import—"refused?"

Dwight growled, his teeth snapping shut a fraction of an inch from the villain's throat.

"Whatever you say," the villain allowed. "I mean, perhaps it is time for a"—Dread halted uncertainly—"change of scene."

At the dog's urging, the criminal mastermind got to his hands and knees and crawled quickly from the bar, surrounded by Delores, Louie, Zabana, Officer O'Clanrahan,

Dwight, and Doc. Further interference from Dread's hench-people was discouraged by two six-guns, a police special, and a strong set of canine teeth, all aimed at their leader.

The door slammed shut behind them, and they were out on the street, in the eternal night.

Delores looked admiringly at Big Louie. "You got us out of there."

Louie blushed. "Well, it wasn't me, exactly."

"Don't be so bashful. I didn't know you had it in you." She gave the sidekick a hearty pat on the back.

"I don't," Louie admitted. "It was Dwight."

"The dog?" Delores asked, not quite comprehending.

"Bark, bark. Yip bark bark," Dwight replied.

"Beg pardon, missy," Doc interrupted. "But it might be better to do our congratulatin' later. We have a bar full of angry fellas behind us here."

"Right you are, boyo!" Officer O'Clanrahan agreed as angry shouts accompanied the sounds of stomping feet from within the bar. "Leave it to a local. I know every back way there is hereabouts." He pointed to an alleyway across the street. "Down there! Quickly!"

Delores frowned at the still-crouched Doctor Dread. "Za-bana? Would you mind carrying our reluctant guest?"

Dread looked up angrily from his crouch, as if he might hesitate meaningfully in obeying Delores' orders. However, the combined proximity of dog fang and jungle muscle kept the villain's complaints to a subverbal level as Zabana lifted him with a single hand.

"Jungle prince at your service!" Zabana announced as he hoisted the snakeskin-suited miscreant over his head.

"Good enough," Delores agreed. "Let's get out of here!"

They followed Officer O'Clanrahan and Dwight into the alley. It was a very dark alley. Where harsh white light seemed to be everywhere on the nighttime streets, here it pooled every fifty feet or so beneath pitifully dim bulbs set high up on the brick walls, leaving the spaces in between totally devoid of illumination. Dwight barked occasionally to let the rest of them know that he and Officer O'Clanrahan were still in the lead. But Delores didn't like walking into the utter darkness. It was like stepping into the void, a place beyond the Cineverse, where there were no more movie worlds, where there was nothing—except nothingness. She had a sudden, chilling thought: If the Change changed everything again, would this be the final result? Would the Cineverse itself cease to exist?

Delores forced herself to breathe regularly, and to keep on walking. She had to admit it. There was only one reason for her thoughts to wander to such depressing extremes. She was still jumpy from her last confrontation in the dark. It was a foolish fear. There wasn't going to be a slime creature waiting for her in every dark place she ever walked into. There couldn't be.

"I've been waiting for you," the deep voice moaned out of the darkness.

Delores only jumped a little bit. After all, she had been expecting this.

"I guess that you have not been waiting for me," the voice said dolefully. "I realize that, at first, the thought of me might be repulsive, nauseating, malodorous, and likely to cause people of a gentle constitution to lose their lunches. But I can be patient. Believe me"—the creature sighed soulfully—"I do grow on people. I have to—it's the fungus in the slime."

"Oh, no!" Dread exclaimed from where Zabana carried him over one jungle-prince shoulder. "It's not—It's not—"

"It is," the Slime Monster reassured him.

Dread screamed.

"He faint," Zabana remarked. "Dead weight on shoulder."

"Such is the memory of slime," the monster commented.

"Now, see here!" Delores demanded. "We have no time for this!" Her patience was at an end. Not only was this monster threatening them, but Big Bertha and the many minions could find them at any minute! Delores hesitated before she spoke again, but realized she had to ask it, even though she knew she didn't want to hear the answer.

"What do you want?"

"I want to give you a choice," the voice said calmly. "You may come with me, and live with me in eternal, if somewhat messy, bliss. So I am mildly radioactive. So what? Why can't I be loved?"

The creature lapsed into a gloomy silence.

"Or?" Delores prompted after a moment.

"Or," the monster sadly continued. "I will be forced to drown you and your fellows in a suffocating wall of slime. You see, we monsters are not accustomed to taking 'no' for an answer."

The voice in the darkness paused, waiting for an answer Delores could not give.

The tension was broken by a voice calling out in a happy Irish brogue:

"Hey, there, boyos! We were almost to the station house when we realized you weren't taggin' along behind. What's takin' so long?"

"Bark bark!" Dwight warned. "Yip bark arf!"

"Say," the Slime Monster asked, "isn't that Dwight the Wonder Dog?"

"Everybody knows Dwight the Wonder Dog!" Officer O'Clanrahan agreed.

"It would be a shame," the monster replied, "if Dwight the Wonder Dog had to be covered by slime."

"Bark, growl!" Dwight replied. "Growl, growl, arf!"

"Yeah, fella," Louie agreed. "But mightn't that be a little dangerous?"

The dog had no chance to answer, for, at that moment, Big Bertha's voice shouted down the alleyway.

"I can hear them up there somewhere. Has everybody got their guns?"

Far too many voices shouted affirmatively.

"How about the bazookas? The flame throwers? The antitank weapons?" Bertha chuckled as other voices yelled their assent. "This time, we're ready for them!"

Two hundred pounding feet echoed down the alleyway.

"You must go," the monster's voice spoke from the darkness. "I will stop them."

"Go?" Delores asked in surprise. "All of us?"

"All of you," the monster agreed. "I sometimes have trouble controlling the direction of my slime."

"What do you say, missy?" Doc asked. "I say we're gone. Thanks a lot, big fella!"

"Think nothing of it," the monster replied. "I always save those things that are mine."

Delores and the others hurried down the alleyway, with Dwight the Wonder Dog leading the way. Behind them, Delores could hear gunfire mixed with shrieks of nausea and disgust, and the ever-present sloshing of heavy liquid.

They paused beneath one of the too-dim lights.

"Where now?" Delores asked as she repressed a shudder.

"Isn't it obvious, young miss?" Officer O'Clanrahan replied. "Doctor Dread has broken every law ever written in this city. I say we should take this felon to the station, and book him!"

"Bark, yip, bark!" Dwight interjected. "Arf, arf, arf!"

"The dog's right," Louie agreed. "This isn't a matter of law and order for a single city, or a single world. This concerns the entire future of the Cineverse!"

"The *dog's* right?" Delores asked in disbelief.

"Arf arf bark!" Dwight added. "Bark, bark, arf bark!"

"It's a good point," Louie mused. "No jail could hold Dread against the force of his minions. But what if we don't put him in jail here? What if we take him to someplace else altogether?"

"Bark yip arf!" Dwight chorused.

"My thought exactly," Louie agreed.

"Eh?" Dread murmured from his resting place on Zabana's shoulder. "No, Mother, don't take my teddy—" He blinked. "Where am I? What happened?" He blinked again, a frown of distaste crossing his countenance. "Slime."

"But that's all behind you now," Doc assured the supervillain. "You're too important to us to leave with a monster."

"That's very—reassuring," Dread managed. "Not that you'll get—anything from me!"

"You call that gratitude?" Zabana asked. "Maybe we take him back to monster!"

"Well," Dread added hurriedly, "I suppose it would do no—harm if I revealed a facet or two of my—master plan. It is too—late for you to stop me, anyway. My plan is moving even—faster than I had hoped, thanks in part to those—extra rings we received from a—former friend of yours."

Extra rings? Former friend? Could Dread be talking about Roger? Delores swore, if that villain had done anything to that sweet man of hers, he would pay.

"I think you will tell us more than that," Louie remarked casually.

"And why do you feel that—little man?" Dread leered. "Do you think to frighten me again? I—assure you, my recent actions were nothing but a momentary—aberration. Now that I have my wits about me, I can truly pledge that I am afraid of—nothing."

"Yip bark yip!" Dwight yapped up at the villain.

"I think so too," Louie said. "It's time to get out of here. If Delores would be so good as to hand me the ring?"

Delores did as she was asked. This, then, must be what Louie had planned all along.

"Whoever's coming, hold on!" Louie instructed. "See you in the funny papers!"

The usual occurred.

When the smoke cleared, Delores gasped.

Never, in her wildest imagination, had she thought the sidekick would bring them here. Was Louie out of his mind?

Doctor Dread started to scream.

⟵ 7 ⟶
"Return of Flaming Death!"

Aaoogah! the sirens wailed. *Aaoogah!*

"Quick, Roger!" Dr. Davenport shouted over her shoulder. "We must get to the main computer!"

Roger nodded as he ran after her through the endless white corridors. Each door they passed was posted with a large, neatly lettered sign: MISSILE ASSEMBLY; FOURTH DIMENSION LAB; ROCKET-TESTING STRIP; ANTIMATTER GENERATOR. Roger really didn't know what help he could be. What did he know about computers?—especially the kind in fifties' monster movies, with all those tape reels and flashing lights. Heck, he had his own desktop computer at work, and, except for the word processing program, he never could figure out how to do *anything* on it.

Still, he had survived worse things in the Cineverse than computer illiteracy. He followed Dee Dee through an opaque glass door marked MAIN COMPUTER.

The room was filled, floor to ceiling, with all sorts of metal hardware. Every inch of space was crammed with gauges, dials, switches, tape reels, and yards and yards of flashing lights, all of it gleaming dully beneath the overhead fluorescents. The sirens were even louder in here. A short, stocky man in a white lab coat ran back and forth across the room, punching a button here, throwing a switch there. All his efforts had no discernible effect. The sirens continued to wail.

"Professor MacPhee!" Dr. Davenport called over the incessant "Aaoogahs." "What's wrong?"

The professor spun to face the newcomers. His round face, neatly bisected by a severely trimmed mustache, nodded distractedly at Dr. Davenport.

"What's wrong?" He laughed harshly. "What isn't wrong?" He waved at the bank of lights to his left. "I guess I realized something was amiss when I first noticed we were getting the Ittelson Effect on our Boatner Board!"

Aaoogah, aaoogah! went the sirens. Red lights flashed on one wall, green lights on another.

"I see," Davenport replied. "But did you try—"

"The Carver Switch?" MacPhee nodded unhappily. "It's the first thing I thought of, what with the possibility of reversed impedance in the Aldridge circuits. But, when all the polarities checked out negative, I was forced to do a reading on the Bollesometer."

"That only made sense," Davenport agreed. "It's a central concern of Young's theorem—"

"Yes, but the reading was totally in the red zone!" MacPhee replied hoarsely.

"Over one thousand bolles per second?" the doctor asked incredulously.

MacPhee nodded. "I'm afraid we're going to prove Young's theorem by blowing up the Institute." Yellow lights flashed on the computer's upper reaches, while white lights blinked near the floor.

Aaoogah! the sirens reminded them. *Aaoogah!*

"Not necessarily!" Dee Dee disagreed. "You remember the work done by Dr. Nordstrom of Helsinki—"

"But that's even more highly theoretical than Professor Young's work!" MacPhee objected.

Dr. Davenport looked at both MacPhee and Roger, her jaw set very stern and square. "Well, I think we're going to prove both of those theorems now, one way or the other. Are you men with me?"

Both men hastily agreed. Roger, as usual, had no idea what was really happening, but in this particular case, he decided that ignorance might be preferable.

Aaoogah! Aaoogah! the sirens screamed. Blue lights rippled across the computer's midsection, crisscrossing the orange lights that flickered around the tape reels.

"Then let's get to work," Davenport commanded. "Once we get the bolles vibrations down to an acceptable level—"

"Under one twenty?" MacPhee asked.

"It'll probably be safe at one fifty, but we'll get it down below one hundred if we can." She slapped both men on the back. "Roger, you'll have to set the Carver Switch to three point six. That's the most the system can take after we've reversed the Aldridge nodules. And when I say 'now,' slowly pull the lever down to zero. Professor MacPhee? It's up to you to man the Fernstetter."

"But that means—" the professor began.

Davenport cut him off abruptly. "That I'll have to override the Roberts Drive? Somebody's got to do it, and, after all, I'm the one who built this baby." She nodded to both of them one final time. "Of course, I don't have to tell either of you the consequences of failure."

"I know," MacPhee replied, his voice barely above a whisper. "Total Bowkerization."

"To your stations," Dee Dee ordered.

Roger was about to ask where and what a Carver Switch was, when he saw the large cardboard sign to his left with four-inch-high letters:

CARVER SWITCH

He walked quickly over to the sign and set the knob

beneath it to 3.6. MacPhee, in the meantime, had grabbed a steering wheel beneath a sign that read FERNSTETTER. Dr. Dee Dee Davenport was on the far side of the room, rapidly punching buttons. Above her head was a large half-circle meter with a sign that read BOLLESOMETER. The indicator in the meter was well into the red zone; over a thousand bolles!

But the narrow pointer on the meter was starting to fall, edging from red to white.

"The Carver Switch is doing its job!" Davenport shouted triumphantly. "Now, if we can only control the vibration effect—"

Aaoogah! Aaoogah! the sirens reminded them. The flashing red lights turned to green, but the blinking green lights changed to red.

That's when the room began to shake. Roger looked up from the trembling switch he still held with his sweating palm. Should this be happening? The Bollesometer was reading less than 300!

Dr. Davenport was nonplussed. "Professor! Double the ratio! And Roger, start turning that dial—NOW!"

The vibrations became even worse, as if the computer control room were at the center of an earthquake. Roger's hand was so damp with sweat that it almost slipped off the knob. But he gripped the Carver Switch with all his might, blinking back the perspiration that fell into his eyes, doing his best to make sure the dial continued its slow, steady descent.

"Now, Professor!" the doctor ordered. "Go to maximum thrust!"

The Fernstetter made a high, whining sound as MacPhee pressed down on the steering column. Roger took a deep breath and turned the Carver Switch as far as it would go, all the way to zero.

Aaoogh—The sirens stopped abruptly. The Fernstetter powered down immediately as well. There was no sound in the room, save for the quiet hiss of rolling tape, the occasional pleasant beeping that accompanied some of the more special lights, and the ragged breathing of the three survivors.

"Gentlemen," Dr. Davenport announced. "We've saved the Nucleotron."

"Thank goodness you were here, Doctor!" MacPhee enthused. "I couldn't have done it by myself."

"Of course not," Davenport agreed. "But what exactly did happen?"

Professor MacPhee bristled at the very thought.

"You know what they would have said if we had failed: 'There are certain things that man was not meant to know.'"

"Yes, but we did not fail," Davenport cajoled. "Although I do understand that the slime monster has broken loose?"

"And 'A scientist should not tempt forces beyond his control!'" MacPhee insisted.

"Yes, but, those forces remained within our control," Davenport said patiently. "Now, about the Slime Monster?"

"Perhaps," MacPhee continued, becoming even more infuriated, "even that 'we should have thought twice before tampering with the very fabric of the cosmos.'" His fingers curled into fists as he looked wildly about the computer room. "Simple-minded fools! Whatever we do, we do for science!"

"Yes, certainly; you'll get no argument on that. But how did the Slime Monster get loose?"

"Oh, that," MacPhee replied, making a visible effort to calm himself. "I'm not too sure—"

Roger frowned. There was something about this fellow that he didn't quite trust. Perhaps it was his agitated manner, always jumping from object to object or topic to topic. Perhaps it was the way he looked through Roger, as if the latter wasn't even there. Or perhaps it was that MacPhee sported a pencil-thin mustache.

Roger knew that he shouldn't judge people on appear-

ance, even in the Cineverse. Simply because both Doctor
Dread and Menge the Merciless had pencil-thin mustaches
was no reason to condemn MacPhee out of hand. The significance of the well-manicured mustache in a fifties' monster world was probably entirely different from its meaning
in, say, a forties' crime setting. Still, the associations
brought to mind by the facial hair were, to say the least,
unsettling.

"Well, what did your instruments tell you?" Davenport
prompted.

"Well, I did mention the Boatner Board and the Ittelson
Effect," MacPhee said defensively.

"Yes, certainly," Davenport replied, her tone suddenly
changing. "Surely something like that must have been at
fault. I'm sorry, Professor. You must be awfully tired from
your recent ordeal. Why don't you take a break? Roger and
I can watch the computer room for a while."

"Do you think so?" MacPhee asked in obvious relief.
"Well, I could use a breather. If you'll excuse me?"

And with that, he was gone.

"I think we could all use a rest," Dr. Davenport admitted.
"A lot has happened to us in the past few minutes."

Roger studied the scientist standing beside him. He wondered if he should ask the obvious question that had sat in
his brain ever since they had escaped the sand and surf.

"You're probably wondering," Dr. Davenport said after
a moment's silence, "how I could be two such different
people on two different worlds. It's one of the secrets of
the Cineverse, and one of the things we study at this Institute
of Very Advanced Science. Still, it's painful to think of
what I had become. I shall never be able to hear a giggle
again without shivering."

She paused to fish in the pockets of her lab coat, finally
pulling out a crumpled pack of cigarettes. "Still, Dr. Davenport and beach bunny Dee Dee are one and the same."

She shook a cigarette free and stuck it in the corner of
her mouth, then offered the pack to Roger. He politely

refused. She fished in the pockets again and found a slim rectangular lighter. "As I said, it is one of the secrets of the Cineverse—and one we were pursuing at the Institute! There are certain worlds, we have found, where you will find yourself in immediate danger; there are other worlds that you or I might consider paradise. But for every single person in the Cineverse, it seems, there is a special world— a world where that man or woman belongs all too much." She paused to light the cigarette. She took a long, nervous drag, then blew the smoke toward the ceiling. "Oh, how I remember that sand and surf and sun, and that relentless surfing beat! Part of me wants to go back there even now. More than that. Part of me *needs* to go back there." She stared down at the glowing end of her cigarette for an instant before going on. "It was like an addiction. I was—" She cleared her throat. "I *am* a beachaholic!"

"A beachaholic?"

Dr. Davenport puffed on her cigarette for a moment, her eyes focused somewhere far away, perhaps on a place where summer never ended. "It was a pleasant enough life, I guess. If you hadn't rescued me, I would have wanted nothing more for the rest of my sunbathing, go-go dancing days." She shivered and looked around for an ashtray.

"I'll always have to live with that, you know—the fact that, on some level, that was the world where I belonged. It's difficult, sometimes, to confront your true self; to look in the mirror and see a blond beach bunny in a bikini. My mind wants to test the limits of science, but my body and soul want to frug throughout eternity!"

She found the ashtray on a small shelf immediately below the Carver Switch. She flicked off the ash, then stubbed out the cigarette. "Ironically, that was one of the subjects we were studying here at the Institute—the hidden relationships between personality type and movie world. As highly theoretical as all this was, we'd even come up with a name for it—Movie Magic."

"Movie Magic?" Roger repeated, despite himself. He

remembered Louie's stories, and his own experiences, with this primal force of the Cineverse. But could there really be a scientific explanation for all of this?

Dr. Davenport struck her fist into her open palm. "There's so much about the Cineverse that we still don't know!" She looked down at her closed fist and laughed ruefully. "I had no idea, when I went to search for the origins of the Slime Monster, that I would stumble into my own personal experiment!"

She looked around the room. The whirring, blinking, and clicking of the great computer seemed to calm her. "But all that's behind me now. I can return to my work, guiding research here at the Institute. What do you think of our computer? It's the very latest design; it can compute complex mathematical equations in mere seconds. And that's only the beginning! Someday, computers will manage many of the mundane aspects of our everyday existence, leaving mankind free to pursue loftier goals. Of course, those computers will have to be much larger than our prototype here, taking up whole city blocks—but I digress."

She leaned closer to Roger, frown lines etched deep into her tanned forehead. "What is your opinion of Professor MacPhee?"

Roger was a bit taken aback. Did Dr. Davenport also distrust the man with the pencil-thin mustache? He wondered how candid he could be concerning an Institute employee he didn't even know. He decided, after a few seconds' thought, to act in the best public relations tradition, with the exact proper mixture of honesty and politeness:

"He did seem a bit evasive."

"I thought so, too," the doctor agreed. "Especially since I can't see how the monster's escape could have possibly affected the Boatner Board. Still, I have been away from the Institute for quite some time. Perhaps there are changes here that I am not yet aware of." She paused, her voice taking on a wistful edge. "There were other reasons for my going on that ill-advised field trip, you know. I also hoped, somehow, to find my father, the brilliant scientist who founded this Institute.''

She paused, her eyes again focused somewhere far away. ''One day, when all this strangeness first began, he came to me and said something very odd, just before he disappeared in a puff of blue smoke. I never saw him again after that moment.''

''Something odd?'' Roger asked, telling himself to stay calm. But what if both of them were looking for the same thing? ''If it's not too personal, could you tell me what it was?''

''I wrote it down,'' she said as she fished inside her plastic pocket pen protector, ''so I wouldn't forget it.'' She pulled out a well-creased piece of paper and unfolded it. ''Here it is. There were two separate thoughts. The first one makes some sense. The second one, though—''

''May I?'' Roger asked, holding out his hand.

She passed the paper to him. His heart raced as he read the neatly printed words:

1. SCIENCE IS THE CORNERSTONE OF TOMORROW'S SOCIETY.

2. ROUGHAGE IS YOUR STOMACH'S BEST FRIEND.

Roger recognized the tone of these messages. After all, he'd seen them spelled out in secret code on a thousand cereal boxes. This could mean only one thing.

''Roger?'' Dr. Davenport asked as she studied the look on his face. ''Is it that terrible?''

''Oh, no, not at all.'' He tried to smile reassuringly as he handed the paper back to her. ''It's just that I've seen messages like these before. I think your father may have had a—how can I put it?—a secret identity.''

The doctor did not seem reassured. ''What do you mean?''

''Have you ever heard of—Captain Crusader?'' Roger asked gently.

She nodded distractedly. ''Why, of course. Every school child in the Cineverse has. But I had always considered him a legend. I had certainly never seen any hard scientific evidence of his existence."

Roger smiled at that; it only made sense. "I'm sure that's the way your father wanted it. He could use this world, and the Institute that he founded here, as a safe retreat from his battles in more violent realms of the Cineverse. And he could use the resources of this establishment of Very Advanced Science to perform the crime-fighting research he needed for his cause. The more I think about it, the more I'm certain." He allowed his smile to widen to a grin as he announced: "Dr. Davenport, your father is Captain Crusader."

"My mother always thought highly of him," Dee Dee agreed, still a bit uncertain. "Yet it is a bit of a shock, finding out your father is a hero among heroes." She looked again at the piece of paper in her hand. "Of course, it would go a long way towards explaining the blue smoke."

Roger shook his head. "What a coincidence that I should rescue the daughter of Captain Crusader! Unless it isn't a coincidence at all. I can't help but feel that everything that has been happening around me, perhaps around all of us, is somehow interconnected. If only I could figure out how— or why."

"It's interesting you should make that point," Dr. Davenport agreed. "It's one of the main fields of research that we at the Institute of Very Advanced Science have put our resources behind. Why, did you know that before my father disappeared in a cloud of blue smoke, we weren't even certain of the existence of the Cineverse? Oh, we knew about it from folk tales, and there was the occasional report of blue smoke, although our armed forces liked to dismiss those sightings, saying they were either swamp gas or weather balloons.

"I suppose I should have given this back to you already." She reached in the pocket of her lab coat and pulled out Roger's ring. "You know, we had to design one of those things ourselves, from scratch. Here—I'll show you the results." She walked over to one of the control consoles and flicked a switch. "Look up at that television screen."

A panel slid aside high on one of the metal walls, to reveal what Roger thought of as a video monitor. The screen showed a blurred, circular image. Dee Dee twisted a pair of knobs on the controls. The image came into focus. It was a Captain Crusader Decoder Ring!

"You can see the problems we had," she explained as she looked down at Roger's ring, still in her hand. "I suppose it was rather like trying to reconstruct an extinct animal from its fossil remains." She pointed back to the television. "See, we thought it should be made in one continuous piece, not broken in four. And we completely missed the concept of chewing gum as an adhesive!"

Roger cleared his throat, and attempted to explain that his ring was not in perfect working order. As a part of his explanation, he managed to fill her in on much of what had happened to him during his adventures in the Cineverse. Occasionally, she would interject a comment to determine if she fully understood him, usually words or short phrases such as "Sidekicks?" "Nut Crunchies?" or "The Secret Samoan?" But for the most part, she only listened politely.

"So you see," Roger concluded, "that's how it happened, in a nutshell."

"Now I see what you mean when you say all you've been through is more than coincidence," was her reply. "Certainly the plans of this so-called Dr. Dread suggest there exists some sort of master plan, if only because that is the plan Dr. Dread is attempting to subvert. And your part in it seems assured by the fact that Dread sent one of his assistants to eliminate you." She paused, and her eyes wandered to the Fernstetter. "I wonder if Dread has sent assistants to sabotage any other part of the Cineverse."

Roger followed her gaze. He remembered who had most recently driven the Fernstetter; the same man who had been alone in this room when the Nucleotron had gone out of control! "Do you mean—"

"I'm afraid I do," she agreed. "I don't think the Slime Monster escaped. I think he was released. And I think someone caused a crisis in the Nucleotron to cover his actions!"

"How clever of you!" a voice called from the doorway. "How fortunate that I decided to stay within earshot of your conversation."

"Professor MacPhee!" Dr. Davenport exclaimed.

The professor stepped into the room, his silver revolver pointed in their direction.

"Or so I have been called around here," MacPhee allowed with the slightest hint of a smile. "But I am sometimes known by another name. Perhaps you've heard of—the Insidious Professor Peril!"

"Professor Peril!" Roger knew that name all too well. Not that he had seen him time and again, as he had with Menge the Merciless. No, but Roger remembered the name from a dozen articles in those nostalgia magazines he used to read about really obscure, grade Z films; articles complete with stills of the professor with Mort the Killer Robot, or Diablo, the Gorilla with the Mind of a Man! Oh, if only Roger had been better versed in minor, extremely low-budget action serials!

"Yes," the poverty-row fiend continued, "I was sent here by Doctor Dread, to make certain that the Institute did not interfere with his plans! Now that you have discovered my true purpose, of course, I am afraid that you will have to be eliminated. But I am not one to talk. I am one to act! If you will come with me?" His pencil-thin mustache twitched as he waved his gun toward the door.

He followed them out into the hall. "If you would please keep on moving. Now, let's see. That's one of the nice things about the Institute. There's so many handy ways to die. Ah, the very place! I think that even Doctor Dread would appreciate the drama of this."

He opened the door marked ROCKET-TESTING STRIP.

"Now, if you would precede me?"

Roger and Dee Dee stepped out into what appeared to be

a very large backyard. There, stretching away from him, as far as Roger could see, were rockets of all shapes and sizes, in all stages of assembly.

Professor Peril glanced around the yard. "Ah, yes. I think this large one over here will do quite nicely. And how providentially coincidental that the workmen have left this large quantity of steel cable lying about. How ideal for tying the two of you to the instrument of your death."

He instructed his two victims to stand against the rocket, which was bright red and sitting on its side, atop a railroad car that in turn was sitting on a set of tracks.

"Now, to properly secure you," Peril continued matter-of-factly. "To do this, I will, of course, have to put my gun between my teeth. I feel it only fair to warn you, however, that I am an excellent shot with my tongue."

No-nonsense villain that he was, Peril had both of them tied securely to the rocket in a matter of seconds.

"Now, I merely have to press the start button on this nearby control board, and the rocket engines will fire. Not that you're taking off anywhere—oh, no. The rocket will instead speed down the tracks to a target a mile or so distant, a concrete wall of sufficient thickness to incinerate the warhead mounted atop your very last ride. You will, of course, be instantly incinerated at some thousands of degrees, a temperature so hot that there will be no remains to be identified. And now, I must be going. I'd chat with you longer, but I haven't time."

The professor trotted over to the nearby control board and pressed the button beneath the large sign that read START. He didn't even wave as he walked smartly back into the Institute.

"Roger?" Dr. Davenport cried from where she was tied beside him. "What can we do?"

Roger looked about wildly. Wait a moment! They were not alone. While the rocket-testing grounds stretched out before them, they were bordered on the right by the backyards of the suburban houses on the adjacent street.

There, not twenty yards distant, two men and a woman stared at them over a white picket fence. The men wore gray flannel suits, the woman a starched white blouse and a full navy skirt covered by a gingham apron.

"Excuse me?" Roger called. "You there?"

The rocket grumbled to life beneath them.

"There are certain things that man was not meant to know," the first fellow commented to the others.

"We could use some help!" Roger added.

The first flickers of flame erupted beneath Roger's feet.

"Indeed," the second agreed. "Scientists should never experiment with forces beyond their control."

"Are you just going to stand there?" Roger asked in desperation. The rocket began rolling down the tracks.

The woman sighed as she glanced at her companions. "They should have thought twice before tampering with the very fabric of the cosmos."

And with a great roar, the rocket picked up speed, carrying Roger and Dee Dee straight toward the concrete wall.

"Do you think," the woman added as an afterthought, "it would do any good to complain about the noise?"

They would be burned alive in a matter of seconds. There was only one chance.

"Do you still have the ring?" he called out over the rocket's roar.

"Oh, yes!" Dr. Davenport shouted back. "It's still in my pocket!"

"Use it!" Roger yelled.

The wind whistled past their ears.

"Well—" she grunted, "if I can get it—"

Roger felt himself being flattened against the rocket's metal hull. He forced his head up, so that he could look past the rocket's nose. There, in the distance, but approaching all too rapidly, was a long gray wall.

They were surrounded by blue smoke.

An instant later, the rocket motors choked off abruptly, replaced by the sound of crashing waves.

"See, I told you they'd come back!" a voice shouted triumphantly.

The smoke cleared, and they were surrounded by sun, and sand, and surf.

"Oh, yeah?" Sneer shot back before the Mad Mumbler could say anything. "Well, this time, they're never going to leave—ever!"

Back on the surfing world? How could this be?

"Oh, no!" Roger shouted from where he was still strapped to the now sand-covered rocket. "Dr. Davenport! What should we do?"

"Tee hee hee," Dr. Davenport replied.

8

"Animated Assault!"

"Jumpin' Jehoshaphat!" Doc exclaimed. "Where in tarnation are we?"

"Trust me," Big Louie said reassuringly. "This is where we want to be."

"No!" Dr. Dread shrieked. "Anywhere but here!"

"It not look real," Zabana remarked. "It look—drawn."

"Exactly," Delores whispered. They were in the middle of a forest somewhere, but no forest that they had ever seen before. Zabana was right. It was as if they had stepped into the middle of a drawing, with the texture of grass and leaves and the bark of trees suggested by pen strokes, all filled in by colors much too bright to come from nature. And it was worse than that. She looked at all her fellows, then down at her own hands, solid flesh-tones now outlined by deep black borders. Not only had their surroundings changed, but they had changed as well.

"We've come to an animated world," she announced. "And we ourselves are animated!"

80

"Bark bark yip arf!" the newly drawn Dwight the Wonder Dog suggested.

"Actually," Louie translated, "Dwight thinks we're rotoscoped."

"Look!" a high-pitched voice called from somewhere out among the trees. "We've got visitors!"

"No!" Doctor Dread screamed as he struggled futilely in the grip of the jungle prince. "Not them! Anything but them!"

Something small and brown and fluffy jumped from behind a bush.

"It bunny rabbit!" Zabana exclaimed.

"How cute!" Delores added, unable to help herself.

"How terrible!" Dread interjected as he stopped struggling and started to shake. "This can't be happening!"

The newcomer wriggled its nose in Dread's direction, then spoke in that same high, clear voice that had come from the trees. "And not just any bunny rabbit. My name's Bigears. I'm the leader of the pack." The rabbit waved an adorable pink paw. "Say, isn't that Dwight the Wonder Dog?"

"Bark bark, yip!" Dwight answered cheerfully.

"Everybody knows Dwight the Wonder Dog!" Officer O'Clanrahan added animatedly.

"*Urk*—" Dread grimaced as if in pain.

"Hey, maybe some of my buddies would like to meet Dwight the Wonder Dog," Bigears suggested. "What do you say, guys?"

"There even more bunnies?" Zabana inquired.

"Hey, there's rabbits all over the place," Bigears replied proudly. "You've landed in Bunnyland!"

"*Gork*—" Dread looked as if he might lose his lunch.

Another pair of bunnies, one gray, one white, came hopping out of the woods.

"Here's a couple of my pals," Bigears explained. "Meet Pinknose"—the white rabbit took a hop in their direction—

"and Fluffytail!" The gray rabbit followed suit.

"*Gurp!*" Dread seemed to be having some sort of spasm.

"Wow," Delores replied, unable to keep the wonder from her voice. "All these bunnies. Is this where—Thumper lives?"

"Nah," the first bunny said deprecatingly. "He's got a contract with another studio. Got a swelled head, won't even write to his old buddies. We've still got some of his relatives, though." He raised his voice to call back to the bushes. "Hey, is Thumper's cousin around here somewhere?"

"Sure!" a much deeper voice answered. "Be right dere!"

The ground shook as the bushes parted.

"*Grork!*" Dread remarked. All the other newcomers, Dwight included, gasped collectively as a very, very large rabbit stepped out into the clearing. This new bunny had regular black and white spots all over its body. However, the most outstanding thing about this rabbit was that it stood some six feet six inches tall.

"Dey call me Bouncer," the very large rabbit announced.

"I can—hold it—no longer!" Dread managed between gritted teeth. "*Gleep! Nerp! Gibber!*"

The supervillain threw his arms in the air, then fell to his knees. His head jerked back, his shoulders forward. His hands twitched, then his feet, followed by his eyebrows and his ears. His snakeskin cowl fell away from his head, and his slicked-back hair stood straight up from his scalp. His eyes rolled rapidly about in their sockets, as his tongue darted in and out of his mouth. There was also smoke coming from his nostrils and inner ears.

That was only the beginning. Everything that was happening to Dread started to happen faster. One moment, he was a mass of twitches and spasms, the next he was moving so quickly that those around him could no longer discern any individual features or limbs—only an indistinct metallic green blur.

"I had no idea it would be this dramatic," Louie whispered.

All of a sudden, Doctor Dread stopped. Now, however, he didn't quite look like Doctor Dread. Perhaps it was those black wizard robes with the golden runes, robes much like the ones Dread had worn when he was about to sacrifice Delores to the Volcano God. Except there was a difference: Now, those robes seemed like they belonged.

"*Nyahahah!*" the reclothed villain remarked.

The rabbits looked up (or, in the case of Bouncer, over) in fright.

"It's Malevelo!" all the bunnies cried together.

The former Doctor Dread whipped something from inside his robes: a foot-long stick with what looked like a cardboard star pasted on the end. At least, Delores thought, that's the way it was drawn.

Dread/Malevelo smiled nastily. "And you'll have to face my Wizard Wand of Wonder! Bunnies, prepare to die!"

The newly created wizard pointed the star-stick at the bunnies. There was an explosion that did not extend as far as the rabbits. When the very dark smoke cleared, black ash covered the wizard's face. He waved the wand again, but it disintegrated in his hand.

"I'll get those dratted rabbits if it's the last thing I do!" Dread/Malevelo shrieked. And with that, the wizard ran off into the forest. As she watched the villain retreat, Delores could swear that the runes across the back of his robes spelled out three words:

SOUVENIR OF BUNNYLAND

The bunnies all laughed merrily.

"Malevelo still hasn't learned!" Bigears exclaimed.

"He keeps trying to get us with his stupid tricks!" Fluffytail added cheerily.

"And they always blow up in his face!" Pinknose cheered as she doubled over with laughter.

"Yeah!" Bouncer asserted. "He should know by now— nobody wins in Bunnyland but bunnies!"

"I knew he was afraid of this place for some reason," Louie admitted with a shiver. "I sure as heck didn't know it was that."

"Yep," Doc replied. "I don't think any of us would have knowingly condemned even someone as rotten as Dread to a fate like—Bunnyland. I mean, it ain't the hero's way."

Even Delores had to admit that she felt sorry for Doctor Dread, if only for an instant. It was basic Cineverse theory that everyone had his own planet of peril, a place where he or she would fit in all too well. Who knew Dr. Dread's perfect fit would be in Bunnyland? But there was no time for misplaced sympathy. They had a job to do.

"Look, men," she said decisively. "We've neutralized Dread. Now all we have to do is find Captain Crusader."

She hesitated. She wished she felt as forceful as she sounded. There was still a part of her that wanted to search for Roger. How were they going to find Captain Crusader, anyway?

Big Louie, as usual, asked her question for her. "How are we going to find Captain Crusader, anyway?"

"No problem there, boyo," Officer O'Clanrahan assured him. "Dwight the Wonder Dog can find anyone."

"Yip bark arf arf!" Dwight agreed.

"Well, it's been awfully nice talking to you," Bigears began cheerfully.

"And meeting Dwight the Wonder Dog!" Pinknose enthused.

"But, now that Malevelo is back, we have things to do," Bigears explained.

"I have to bake some cream pies," Fluffytail agreed.

"The kind that are good for throwing!" Bigears elucidated.

"I'll have to write up some 'This Way to Bunnies' signs," Pinknose volunteered.

"Yeah," Bigears agreed, "he always falls for that one."

"You know what you have to do, Bouncer," Pinknose prompted.

The big rabbit rocked with mirth. "Yeah"—snicker, snicker—"da exploding carrots!"

All the bunnies had a good laugh.

Doc had sidled over to Delores as the rabbits relayed their plans.

"Missy?" he whispered in her ear. "Are you *sure* we shouldn't save him?"

Delores shook her head. "Sometimes, I'm afraid, we have to be pragmatic rather than heroic. It's a part of the Change."

Doc nodded solemnly. "Now I remember why I took to drink."

The bunnies waved a final time as they hopped back into the forest. Delores turned back to the benevolently smiling Officer O'Clanrahan.

"So you want to find Captain Crusader, do you?" he chortled. "Well, all we need to do is take Dwight to the last place you saw that Captain—to get the scent, don't you know. After that, the Wonder Dog will track him anywhere in the Cineverse!"

Delores decided that sounded simple enough. The last place they had seen Captain Crusader was on that island paradise where they were to be sacrificed to the Volcano God. But the Captain, in his guise as the Secret Samoan, had helped to foil that sacrifice before he disappeared.

Then, the island paradise was where they had to go. Delores imagined it would be safe enough there, now that Doctor Dread was no longer present to incite the islanders. She would have to gather the others around her and use the ring at once.

That's when they were surrounded by blue smoke, not to mention diabolical laughter.

"Ah hahahaha! Ah hahahaha!"

Delores would recognize that laugh anywhere. Even without looking at his bald head, pencil-thin mustache, or signature silver space robes, she would have known instantly it was Menge the Merciless!

Dwight growled menacingly as Doc drew his six-guns and Zabana beat his chest in a clear jungle challenge. Louie cleared his throat.

"Uh, don't you think it's time we got out of here?"

"Not so fast, mortals," Menge gloated. "Doctor Dread has put out a distress signal. Soon, every cutthroat in his employ will be converging upon this very spot. You wouldn't want to leave and miss the party? Ah hahahaha! Ah hahahaha!"

Even as he spoke, there was another pair of blue smoke explosions. The larger one was to the left, and—as the cartoon smoke drifted away on the cartoon wind—revealed Big Bertha and her many minions! Delores didn't recognize the short, stocky fellow at the center of the other dissipating cloud, although the robot and gorilla he had brought along certainly looked menacing.

"Say!" the newest villain called out as he pointed to Delores' canine companion. "Isn't that Dwight the Wonder Dog?"

"Ah hahahaha! Ah hahahaha!" was Menge's answer. "Even Dwight the Wonder Dog can't save them now! Heroic fools—there is only one thing in your future! Death!"

And with that, the entire assembled might of Cineverse villainy rushed forward.

⚊ 9 ⚊
"Bombs Away!"

"Hey, what did we tell you!" Brian said to the Motorcycle Mob. "Roger's back, and we've still got eight hours before the Cowabunga-munga!"

Only eight hours? Roger became even more upset. When they'd escaped this place, hadn't there been more than a day? It was a forceful reminder that Cineverse time was different, and somewhat more treacherous, than time on Earth.

"Oh, yeah?" Sneer taunted. "How's he gonna surf if he's tied to that thing?"

The surfers were silent for a second.

"I know what to do!" Frankie shouted. "It's time for a surfing song!"

A surfing song? Roger was still strapped to the rocket ship by the heavy metal cables. There was no way he could escape. What could he do?

"Well, you've got to give Roger this," Brian admitted admiringly. "Whenever he shows up, he sure brings some funky stuff along."

"Yeah?" Sneer jeered. "But is it funky enough to surf?"

Bix Bale and the Belltones took that as their cue. Guitars and drums took up a merry surfing beat.

Frankie started to sing:

> "Roger's strapped to a rocket ship.
> Fella knows how to take a trip!
> He'll go free, now we can't go wrong;
> He brought his salvation along!"

"Hey!" the crowd shouted in unison.

Boom be boom be boom be boom boom boom, the drums replied.

"Nanny nanny-nanny, nanny-nanny hey!" all the surfers chorused.

Brian took the second verse. Roger could already feel his feet tapping.

> "Roger's lucky he's got Dee Dee;
> She's the girl who will set him free!
> She's so cute and she's so svelte;
> A single touch and the knots will melt."

Dr. Davenport giggled and touched the cable. Roger felt the steel cords loosen and slip off his body. The cable fell into the sand with a soft but solid sound.

"Hey!" everybody yelled.

Biff bang boom de boom crash crash boom, the drums responded.

"Nanny nanny-nanny, nanny-nanny hey!" was the general reply, made by surfers, beach bunnies, Bix's band, the Motorcycle Mob, including—somewhat indistinctly—the Mad Mumbler. What could Dee Dee and Roger do but join in?

Roger jumped from the rocket wing, ready to Watusi.

That's when the music changed. Roger paused, mid-twist. He knew what was coming before half a dozen beats had gone by. It was time for the drum solo.

Biff bang boom de boom bif bang bang bang, said the drums.

Roger blinked. He was himself again, free of dance fever. It had something to do with drum solos—you could never dance to them.

Biddeboom, the drums went. Biddeboom biddeboom biddeboom.

Dee Dee, however, wasn't so lucky. She had stopped dancing, but she had turned to face the drummer, and was raptly watching his every move.

Biddeboom boom boom, the drums went. Biddeboom boom boom. Dee Dee jumped up and down excitedly.

If Roger had needed any further proof that Dr. Dee Dee Davenport was totally under the spell of the surfing world, this was it. Nobody could be that interested in a drum solo— unless greater forces were at work.

Boom dedede boom boom, the drums continued. Boom dedede bif boom.

"Dee Dee!" Roger called.

"Tee hee hee," she replied as she bounced up and down.

"We need the ring," he insisted.

She gave him a ditzy stare. "The ring?"

Roger pointed. "In your pocket."

"Pockets? Tee hee hee. Bikinis don't have any pockets, silly!" She looked down at her white lab coat and frowned. "Hey, why am I wearing this fuddy duddy old thing?" She rapidly unbuttoned the coat and shrugged it from her shoulders, revealing the bright green swimsuit beneath. She bunched the coat into a ball and handed it to Roger. "Here. Put this someplace for me, would you? Tee hee hee."

Roger saw something flash in the sun. The ring had fallen out of the pocket.

"Dee Dee!" he called.

But she had seen it, too, and grabbed it before the ring could be lost in the sand.

"Oops," she said.

They were again surrounded by blue smoke.

"Tee. Tee hee. Tee." Dee Dee shivered. "It's so hard to stop."

Roger looked up from where Dr. Davenport huddled beside him. This time, they had materialized directly in front of the Institute. It was night, and there was a chill in the air. He handed her back her white lab coat.

She regained her composure as she buttoned the coat around her. "This time, I think your ring saved us." She offered Roger a wry smile. "Of course, it was probably your ring that got us into trouble in the first place." She waved for Roger to follow her as she marched toward the Institute.

"After all, Roger," she continued as he trotted to catch up with her, "what are the chances, with all the thousands upon thousands of myriad worlds that we might have landed upon in the Cineverse, that both times you hastily used your ring to escape from danger, it deposited you in the exact same place?"

Roger hadn't thought of that. "I would say that the odds are phenomenal against that sort of thing—"

"Unless there was something about the ring that forced that result!" Dr. Davenport finished for him. "You said yourself that you were amazed, when you fixed the ring, that it worked at all. Well, unfortunately, I think it only works now in two very limited ways. When you almost drop it, as I managed to do twice in my beach bunny state, it sends you home. However, should you try to use it in the usual way—"

Roger caught her drift. "—it will deposit you back on that surfing world!"

"Exactly. Your ring, I'm afraid, only retains a very limited usefulness. Not that we should complain, after all. Its use, erratic as it is, is probably the only thing that has kept us alive."

She handed the ring back to Roger. He sighed and put it in his pocket.

"But if we don't have a working ring," he asked, "how can we ever find Captain Crusader?"

Dee Dee opened the door to the Institute. "You mean my father?" She sighed again. "Yes, it would be nice to see him again. There are so many questions I have to ask—especially about the fourth dimensional project." The wistfulness disappeared from her voice as she smiled back at Roger. "But anyway, who said we didn't have a working ring?"

She nodded to the security guard as Roger followed her inside.

"Dr. Davenport!" the security man exclaimed. "I didn't see you go out."

"We didn't, Sweeny," she replied laconically. "At least, not the front way—" She waved Roger past the gate. "You've already met our guest, here. We have to go back to the main computer."

Sweeny nodded and dutifully went back to reading his newspaper.

They walked at a more leisurely pace down the long, white corridor, which gave Roger the chance to read a few more signs that he had missed before: EXPERIMENTAL HYPERDRIVE; ROBOT ASSEMBLY; GIANT INSECT LAB. The more he wandered around this place, the more he had to admit that they practiced some Very Advanced Science at the Institute.

Dr. Davenport once again ushered him through the door marked MAIN COMPUTER. This time, there were no wailing sirens and warning lights; only a giant computer humming happily to itself, its tape reels spinning, its lights blinking away in sensible sequences.

"It's very peaceful in here," Dee Dee remarked, "don't you think? Sometimes a scientist needs a place like this, where she can get away." She took a deep breath, as if she might inhale the very essence of science, then walked over to one of the room's innumerable consoles and punched a series of buttons.

"I'm going to show you something here few people have seen before. It's the latest in very advanced science—we can talk directly to this computer!" She paused for a moment, perhaps to allow the concept to sink in. "Or," she continued, "perhaps I should call our mechanical friend by name. She's known as the Very Educated Research Analyzer—or VERA. Good evening, VERA."

The computer beeped cheerily. Something made a ratcheta-ratcheta sound on the left side of Dee Dee's console. A moment later, a foot or so of paper tape, a bit wider perhaps than the kind Roger was used to seeing in a cash register, spewed out of a slot near eye level. Dee Dee ripped off the tape and handed it to Roger.

GOOD EVENING, DR. DAVENPORT, it read.

"VERA," the doctor continued, "I've brought along an associate who's going to work with us. I'd like you to meet Roger."

Ratcheta-ratcheta, went the console. Another length of paper tape spewed forth.

PLEASED TO MEET YOU, ROGER, it read.

"Likewise, I'm sure," Roger replied, his public relations politeness taking over before he could even consider what way it might be best to address a machine.

Dr. Davenport spoke again. "But we were talking about our experimental device number X-33—what you know as the Captain Crusader Decoder Ring." She punched another button, and the television reappeared high on the wall, complete with ring pictures.

Dr. Davenport started to talk clearly but rapidly, as if she were giving a lecture: "The Decoder Ring, or X-33, is a remarkably delicate device. You've already seen how we determined the basic design with reasonable accuracy. However, it was only when we lowered the grade of plastic sufficiently that the rings began to work." Her fingers flashed across the console, and the picture on the monitor lost most of its shine. "Since then, we have been constantly refining our understanding of the ring's properties. Our major discovery thus far is how much better the rings worked when they were combined for a period of time with what we—at first—considered a hypothetical product: what you would call a breakfast cereal."

"Nut Crunchies?" Roger asked in astonishment.

"I see you're way ahead of me," she replied, obviously impressed. "This cereal concoction turned out to be truly amazing. The sugar glaze that covers Nut Crunchies is simply one of the strongest adhesives known to man. But you probably know that, as well."

Roger shook his head. It was actually something that he had only suspected. Heaven knew, Nut Crunchies had been sweet—and the only thing his twelve-year-old Captain-Crusader-Decoder-Ring-collecting self would eat for breakfast. Without Nut Crunchies in his stomach in the morning, the twelve-year-old Roger had never felt properly hyperactive.

"But, at last," Dr. Davenport continued, "our experimentation was over—and *voilà*!" She punched a final button.

Ratcheta-ratcheta went the console. A length of paper again appeared.

MY PLEASURE, DR. DAVENPORT, it read.

A drawer popped open at waist level before her. Roger peered over her shoulder. The drawer contained only one thing—a perfect replica of a Captain Crusader Decoder Ring!

Dee Dee picked up the ring, a noble yet faraway look in her eye. "We have other problems, of course. There's a slime monster out there somewhere, after all. But, from all you've told me, I think the location of Captain Crusader should be our primary goal. Roger, this ring is for you."

She placed the small circle in Roger's palm. The gray ring was so shiny and new, it looked as if it had just popped out of a box of Nut Crunchies! Roger was speechless.

Dr. Davenport said it for him. "Thank you, VERA."

Ratcheta-ratcheta, the machine replied. Dee Dee ripped off the paper tape.

ANYTHING FOR SCIENCE, it read.

Dr. Davenport nodded pleasantly at the appropriateness of the readout. "Our research has revealed some other things about experiment X-33," she continued. "I realize, of course, from all that you have told me, that time is of the essence. I shall therefore attempt to be as brief as possible. There seems to be more than pure coincidence at work in the combination of these rings and the Nut Crunchie cereal. In fact, certain experiments show that there might even be a strangely symbiotic relationship between the two."

She took a deep breath, as if considering the best way to proceed. "We don't have time for me to review the entire experimental process. I will only tell you about the fortuitous discovery made by one of our researchers when he pressed a single Nut Crunchie into one of our rings and left it overnight on a kitchen table—we've discovered, for some reason, that kitchen tables present the best results when working with these particular materials—Formica-topped tables in festive colors, with little inlaid squiggles of gold and silver."

She stopped herself, the slight smile of scientific discovery disappearing from her lips. "But I digress. About the discovery—Next day, the researcher returned to find that the high sugar content of the Nut Crunchie had somehow permanently bonded itself to the plastic of the Captain Crusader Decoder Ring. But, it had done even more than that—the Nut Crunchie/cheap plastic interface had changed the very nature of the ring's performance!"

She pointed proudly at the ring Roger now held in his hand. "That is such a ring. We've come up with different, special rings for different purposes. Some will take you to special places, much as you inadvertently did with your broken ring. Others can search out individual qualities within the Cineverse; still more can locate recent ring ac-

tivity on nearby worlds. But the most amazing property we
have found is contained in the ring that you hold in your
hand—a quality so profound that one might almost believe
that Captain Crusader himself was somehow responsible.
Or even that some of the other wild legends of the Cineverse
could be true!''

Other legends? Roger wanted to ask her what "wild legends" she referred to, but stopped when he saw her look
of intense concentration.

She bit her lower lip in a gesture that somehow reminded
Roger more of a beach bunny than a respected scientist.
"How can I explain it? Well—we like to call what you
hold in your hand the Ring of Truth."

"The Ring of Truth?" Roger repeated in wonder.

She nodded. "In other words, this ring is customized. I
particularly like the small flame decals the computer placed
on the sides. However, you're probably curious as to what's
special about this ring, which, incidentally, works like any
other Captain Crusader Decoder Ring, except for one important difference."

She paused dramatically.

"Which is?" Roger asked, for he felt it was expected of
him.

"This ring, when used properly," she continued, now
that Roger had done his part, "can force a truthful answer
from anyone. More specifically, that little plastic beauty is
a hero finder! It has been specifically modified for you to
point and ask your suspect if he is indeed Captain Crusader!"

Roger held the ring out at arm's length. "You mean, like
'Are you Captain Crusader?' " he recited uncertainly.

"Yes," Dee Dee agreed. "That's it exactly. Sooner or
later, you're bound to get a positive response to that question, and the man you've searched the Cineverse for will
be revealed!"

Roger looked admiringly down at the specially modified
ring. It seemed simple enough.

"But you're probably wondering," Dee Dee asked, "with all the Cineverse in front of you, how should you begin your search?"

Roger nodded. There was that.

"Well, I have a pair of answers to that. First, thanks to our experiments with the X-33, we at the Institute have compiled a world-by-world guide to the Cineverse. And I have a copy for you!"

She handed him a thick paperback volume, white with red and blue lettering. Roger read the title with a frown:

The Cineverse—From A to Zed

"Don't worry," she reassured him. "Using it is child's play. Now, as to where you should start your search, I have taken the liberty of calling up the Captain Crusader program on VERA, here. Even as we speak, this computer is comparing the statistical probabilities of the various potential locations where Captain Crusader may be at this very second! In a matter of minutes—certainly under half an hour— VERA will send you on the way to that place where Captain Crusader probably is!"

Roger stared at the randomly blinking lights as he and Dee Dee waited for the computer's answer.

"There is so much we still do not know," Dee Dee mused. "Why so many different worlds? Why a cheap plastic ring? Why this odd matching of world and individual—a chemistry, if you will—that causes someone to change the way I did on the beach party planet?" She shuddered very slightly. "I tell you, it almost makes you want to believe in the Plotmaster."

The Plotmaster?

Where had Roger heard that name before? The randomly blinking lights blurred before him, replaced by a haze of blue smoke. Only, this time, it wasn't smoke erupting from a Captain Crusader Decoder Ring—no, it was the languid curl of smoke rising from a large cigar.

The Plotmaster.

Roger blinked, and the smoke was gone. He realized that

the blue haze had never really been there. It had been a vision—of something that had happened but that he was supposed to forget.

There had been four of them: Doc, Zabana, Louie, and himself. And they had become trapped in an endless series of Swashbucklers Louie referred to as a "Cineverse cycle." On one world, someone was trying to unseat a pretender to the throne. On others, Roger and his cohorts faced blood-thirsty pirates, fierce, bloodthirsty swordswomen, and happy, singing, bloodthirsty buccaneers. Roger's band bounced from world to world, unable to escape from the sounds of clashing swords, and coming closer to death with every passing moment.

Until—

Roger remembered the silhouette of the big man with the booming voice; the man with the cigar! The stranger had rescued Roger and his fellows from certain skewering, re-placed their defective Captain Crusader Decoder Ring with another in proper working order, casually mentioned that neither Roger nor his fellows would retain any memory of that particular meeting, and, in conclusion, calmly sug-gested they should all "do lunch" sometime.

Then he had sent them away, back into the Cineverse. They weren't supposed to remember that meeting, or any-thing about him. But for some reason—perhaps because he came from Earth rather than the Cineverse—Roger remem-bered it all.

"The Plotmaster," he whispered in awe.

"That's what I said," Dr. Davenport agreed. "Another unproven hypothesis, one of my wild legends I suppose you could call it, from that vast, unexplored region we call the Cineverse—"

She was interrupted by the ratcheting of the console.

"Ah. Our answer at last." Dr. Davenport ripped off the paper tape.

"Dr. Davenport," Roger began uncertainly. "Dee Dee?

Uh—I know something about this so-called legend—this Plotmaster—''

"Just a moment, Roger.'' The doctor frowned down at the paper in her hands. "There's something wrong here.''

I AM SORRY, DR. DAVENPORT, BUT I CANNOT COMPLY WITH YOUR REQUEST, the paper read.

"Whyever not?'' Dee Dee asked in consternation.

BECAUSE OF MY COUNTERPROGRAMMING, the computer replied after the usual ratcheting.

"Counterprogramming!'' Dr. Davenport demanded. "Who counterprogrammed you?''

PROF. MACPHEE, the machine replied. I'M AFRAID HE IN-STALLED A PENCIL-THIN MUSTACHE, SO YOU WOULD BE DESTROYED.

"No!'' the doctor exclaimed.

YES, the machine replied in no time at all. WITH THE PENCIL-THIN MUSTACHE INSTALLED, I AM COMPELLED TO ACT IN THIS WAY. IT IS ONE OF THE LAWS OF THE CINEVERSE.

"But, there must be some way we can counter-counter-program you!'' Dee Dee objected.

TOO LATE, the computer cautioned. I'M AFRAID THE BOMB WILL HAVE GONE OFF BEFORE YOU CAN DO MUCH OF ANY-THING.

"The bomb?'' She turned to her companion. "Quick, Roger, you must get away from here! Only you can save the Cineverse!''

"But,'' Roger objected, "I can't leave you here alone to face the bomb!''

But Dr. Davenport was adamant. "I'm afraid you have no choice. I can't leave now. That bomb would destroy the Institute, and everything that I have ever worked for. But I can't risk both our lives for what is my dream. Go, Roger, set a course for somewhere out in the Cineverse! You'll find Captain Crusader; I know you will! Ever since you've entered our realm, you've been phenomenally lucky!''

VERA interrupted them by ratcheting one more time.

THE NEW INSTRUCTIONS REQUIRE THAT I SAY ONE FINAL

THING, the computer printout read. NO ONE ESCAPES PRO-FESSOR PERIL!

"Roger, you must go now!" Dr. Davenport insisted. "Set your ring for anywhere. It doesn't matter if you end up in the wrong place. You've got the guidebook now. You can ask directions!"

"But—" Roger began.

"Get out of here!" Dee Dee demanded. "I can't have you hanging around and distracting me."

Well, Roger thought, if that's the way she felt about it. He tucked the Cineverse guidebook into the elastic waistband of his jogging pants, then zipped the bottom of his jacket to make sure the book wouldn't slip out. Once he had his hands free, he twisted the ring. "See you in the funny papers!"

The last thing he heard was the console ratcheting. That, and the sirens starting up again with their *Aoogah, aoogah, aoog*—

He realized, as the blue smoke rose to encircle him, that he had never told Dr. Davenport about the Plotmaster.

But then he was gone.

⊿ 10 ⊿

"No Escape!"

"I'll hold 'em off, missy," Doc announced, "long's my ammunition holds out!"

"Zabana call wild animals," the jungle prince added. "Wait minute. How you call cartoons?"

"I assure you, miss," Officer O'Clanrahan spoke reassuringly, "myself and Dwight the Wonder Dog will demand a full accounting!"

"Wait a minute!" Louie suggested. "Maybe there's a way we can avoid all this."

But Delores realized there was no more time for talk. The villains were upon them. Menge had pulled some sort of ray gun from his silver robes. The evildoer laughed merrily as he pointed the gun at Doc.

That new fellow, his robot and gorilla in tow, was sneaking up behind Zabana. Neither the robot nor the gorilla seemed capable of moving with any speed, but they both appeared capable of quickly strangling the life out of anyone, even a jungle prince. And Zabana seemed unaware of their approach, since he was temporarily preoccupied with finding some way of making his animal rescue calls more animated.

Dwight and Officer O'Clanrahan, in the meantime, were facing up to the hundred henchmen Big Bertha had brought along.

"Bark, growl!" Dwight remarked. "Bark, yip, growl!" The henchmen still approached, slowly but inexorably.

But Delores had other things to worry about. Big Bertha was bearing straight towards her, the gangsterette's expression even more furious than usual.

"Delores!" the very large woman growled. "Do you have any idea how difficult it is to get slime stains out of black vinyl?"

Big Bertha's remarks did nothing but increase Delores' resolve. She was a hero now, after all, and would not be killed over a fashion issue.

"Where is Doctor Dread?" Menge demanded of Doc.

The old Westerner offered a weathered grin. "Well, by cracky, young fella, he's around here somewhere. 'Ceptin' I don't think you'd recognize him."

"That doesn't sound like a straight answer to me!" Big Bertha declared. "Our leader would *deal* with all of them for less than that!"

"Then we should deal with them and get on with it!" the newest villain snapped. "All this sitting around and talking is uneconomical!"

"Hmmm," the silver-suited Menge considered. "I like your style. Very no-nonsense."

"Villainy on a budget," the newcomer agreed.

"Very well!" Menge the Merciless called to all those around him. "Minions of evil! Let's do something a little special, and kill all these worthless do-gooders"—his pregnant pause was worthy of Doctor Dread—"in unison."

"Aren't you forgetting something?" a high-pitched voice called from behind the trees.

"Who's that?" Menge demanded.

"Dr. Dread?" Bertha asked hopefully.

But the high-pitched rabbit voice hadn't finished its speech.

"Nobody kills anybody," it continued, "—in Bunny-land!"

That's when Delores saw them—five-hundred tiny, furry, points; some gray, some black, some white. They rose slowly from the grass all around the heroes and villains, to reveal a thousand pink ears, a thousand rabbit eyes, then five hundred rapidly-twitching pink noses.

"What's going on here?" Menge demanded.

"I think—" Bertha replied haltingly, "that we're sur-rounded—by bunnies!"

"Bunnies?" Menge laughed. "I thought it was something serious!"

"Bunnies are never serious!" Bigears shouted from the back of the pack. "Show 'em, fellas!"

Five hundred pairs of paws lifted five hundred cream pies into view.

"Uh-oh," Big Bertha remarked.

The ground beneath the meadow shook as a very, very large rabbit burst from the trees.

"Bouncer to da rescue!" the very, very large bunny an-nounced. He was carrying something that looked like a very large carrot, except that the vegetable's orange skin shone like polished metal. He stuck the carrot, pointy end first, into Menge the Merciless' ray gun.

"A carrot?" Menge asked.

BOOM! went the carrot, creating a neat little explosion in the archfiend's immediate vicinity. When the smoke cleared, Menge's face and upper body were covered with vast quantities of very dark ash.

He squeezed the trigger of his ray gun. The gun disin-tegrated.

Five hundred bunnies giggled together.

"Uh-oh," Menge replied.

"Let Zabana see," the jungle prince mused, oblivious not only to the robot and gorilla almost upon him, but to the five hundred bunnies as well. "Would it be 'chee chee rabbit rabbit chee?' Or would it be 'chee chee cartoon rabbit cartoon rabbit chee'?"

"Hey, Zabana!" Louie yelled as he kicked the gorilla (which, upon closer inspection, looked more like a guy in a gorilla suit) in the seat of the pants. "You've got company!"

"Company? Zabana like company!" The jungle prince turned to regard the gorilla and the robot (which, upon closer inspection, looked an awful lot like a guy in a robot suit). He smiled. "How you like jungle prince bear hug greeting?"

"And I almost had him!" the newest fellow with the pencil-thin mustache screamed. "I'll show you what I do to people who try to thwart my deadly-yet-economical plans! You do not toy with someone who controls Mort the Killer Robot, and Diablo, the Gorilla with the Mind of a Man. Prepare to face the wrath of Professor Peril!"

But, for now, Professor Peril only stood there and seethed. Delores glanced back at the glowering Big Bertha, then at her many minions, who hesitantly took a step forward; then at the ring of surrounding bunnies, who all lifted their cream pies into better throwing position.

Something was bound to happen very soon.

"I'll get you rabbits yet" a voice called from the edge of the woods.

"Who's that?" Professor Peril called.

Still somewhat frazzled, Menge peered into the distance. "Some old guy in a wizard suit."

"No," Bertha interjected. "I recognize that suit from a certain volcano sacrifice I recently attended. That's not just any old guy in a wizard suit; it's one old guy in a very particular wizard suit!"

"Do you mean—" Professor Peril began hastily.

"But it can't—" Menge the Merciless objected.

Bertha nodded her head sadly. "It most certainly can be—Doctor Dread!"

"I'll get you bunnies if it's the last darned thing I do!" the Dread wizard shouted at the rabbit horde.

"Uh-oh," the hundred minions moaned in unison.

"We have to do something!" Professor Peril insisted. "And we have to do it now!"

That's when things started to happen. Menge, Peril, Bertha, and the many minions all started to run—except for Mort and Diablo, who had a tendency to lumber—in no particular direction. Perhaps they were trying to rescue Doctor Dread from this fate worse than almost anything, perhaps they were simply attempting to escape the deadly pie assault. Whatever they were doing—thanks in large part to the five hundred cream pies, which seemed to be evenly divided between lemon and chocolate—it was a mess.

"I've got him!" Professor Peril shouted from beneath a faceful of whipped cream. "I've got Doctor Dread!"

"What are you talking about!" Dread struggled in Peril's grasp. He might have gotten away, too, if the professor had not quickly handed him over to the collective grasp of Mort the Killer Robot, and Diablo, the Gorilla with the Mind of a Man.

"I am Malevelo!" Dread insisted. "Bane of cartoon rabbits everywhere! I cannot leave here until my job is done— and cute cartoon bunnies are eliminated—forever!"

"Oh boy!" Bouncer chuckled. "Da time has come for more exploding carrots!" He bounded heavily back into the forest.

"I think," Peril spoke economically, "it's time to leave."

"Very well," Menge the Merciless agreed. "The master plan is too far along. Soon, the Change will change our way—forever! There is no way for these heroic incompetents to stop us now! Villainous lackeys, set your rings. We leave to conquer the Cineverse! Ah hahahaha! Ah haha-haha!"

The entire meadow was covered with blue smoke, carried away quickly by the animated wind. The circle of bunnies let out a collective gasp. Not only had all the bad guys, including the wizard-suited Doctor Dread, vanished, but they had taken all remnants of the pie-fight with them as well. There was nothing left in the meadow but green grass and wildflowers, shining in the cartoon sun.

"Nary a crumb," Pinknose remarked.

"And after all that baking!" Fluffytail lamented.

"Don't worry!" Delores called out, automatically reacting to the sight of five hundred depressed cartoon rabbits. "The pies may be gone, but look at the results you've gotten. You've defeated the combined might of the nastiest bunch of villains ever to do evil in the Cineverse!" She paused to wave at the horde of rabbits surrounding her. "Even though we don't know you all by name, I'd like to thank every one of you!"

Bigears slapped his back paws in embarrassment. "That's right, you haven't been properly introduced. How thoughtless of me!" He nodded at the assembled rabbitdom. "Delores, I'd like to introduce my bunny legion."

"Oh, that's quite all right," Delores demurred with a smile. "We must be—"

But the bunny leader wouldn't hear of it. He hopped from rabbit to rabbit, introducing each of his fellows as he landed: "This is Fleckedtail—" Hop. "And Spottyback—" Hop. "And Bentear—"

Big Louie trotted up beside Delores. "Now that Dread's gone, shouldn't we be making tracks, too?"

"—and Pinkeyes," Bigears continued with a hop. "And Graywhiskers—" Hop. "And Threepaws—" Hop.

"To let Dwight sniff out Captain Crusader? My thought exactly," Delores agreed. "But can we get there from here?"

"And Brownnose—" the rabbit continued as it hopped, "and Notail—" Hop. "And Crosseyes—" Hop. "And Tallears—"

"The Volcano world?" Louie mused. "Sure. No problem."

"And Bigfeet—"

"You can find it with the ring?" Delores asked.

"And Highjumper—" Hop. "And Pinkears—"

Louie shrugged. "I've got a talent for this sort of thing."

"And Spottypaw—"

"Good," Delores replied tersely. "Get the others together. Now!"

"And Mottlednose—"

"We really must be going," Delores insisted.

"—you already know Fluffytail," Bigears continued, then stopped abruptly, as if Delores' assertion had only then penetrated his bunny brain. "You have to leave? Now?" His ears twitched in consternation. "I still have to introduce you to four hundred and eighty-one bunnies!"

"It certainly is a shame that we have to run," Delores agreed. "I'm sure we'd all be glad to meet every single one of you some other time, when the very fate of the Cineverse wasn't at stake."

"Oh," Bigears replied, trying hard to cover his disappointment. "The very fate of the Cineverse? I guess I can understand—"

"And when we have time, boyo," Officer O'Clanrahan interjected, "I'm sure Dwight would be glad to give every one of your fellow rabbits the Wonder Dog handshake!"

"Bark bark, yip!" Dwight agreed.

"Gee, really?" Bigears marveled. "Well, I guess it's all right, then."

"You learn a lot from doing personal appearances," the officer remarked to Delores in a stage whisper.

"And we'd better be going," Louie announced. "Come on, everybody, grab hold. Next stop—a South Sea paradise!"

All the heroes gathered around. All the bunnies cheered merrily. There was the required blue smoke.

They heard the voice even before the smoke had cleared. Delores remembered that voice.

"Once again, we welcome our happy visitors to our friendly island paradise."

And then the smoke was gone, blown away by the island wind. Delores glanced around at her companions. All of them, save Dwight and O'Clanrahan, appeared tense, no doubt remembering the circumstances of their last visit to this "island paradise."

"Our visitors discover, to their delight, that they are greeted by the peaceful islanders bearing flowers," the sonorous voice continued. Now that the smoke had cleared away completely, Delores could see the speaker—the village elder—smiling beatifically.

"So, it really is peaceful around here?" Louie asked skeptically.

"More peaceful than you could imagine," one of the island maidens replied as she tossed a lei around his head. Did Delores catch a hint of desperation in her tone?

"How Volcano God?" Zabana asked cautiously.

"Oh, quiet as can be," one of the young men of the island replied with a sigh.

"And howsabout those quaint island customs you fellas used to have?" Doc demanded.

"Fallen into disuse," the elder reassured him. "Especially anything to do with knives and sacrifices. So you see, our visitors have nothing to look forward to except for fun under the sun!"

The island men and women groaned en masse.

Delores studied the natives somewhat more carefully. She couldn't shake the feeling that, once again, the village elder was holding something back. If everything was so peaceful around here, why were all the islanders so miserable?

Louie said it for her: "You know, if everything is so peaceful around here, why do all you islanders look so miserable?"

One of the young men ignored the warning frown of the village elder, to blurt out: "Do you know how boring it is with nothing but fun in the sun? Ever since you outsiders left, all the zest has gone out of our plots!"

"Oh, we've done all the standard things," a maiden continued. "You know, a lad from the wrong side of the tribe runs off with the princess."

"We even did a girl from the wrong side of the tribe running off with the prince!" another added.

"But with a limited cast, what else can you do?" the first fellow concluded. "We've had to face it. We've run out of plots."

Delores felt an involuntary shiver run through her body as she saw her companions blanch around her. Run out of plots? In the Cineverse? That was unthinkable! Or, Delores realized, worse than unthinkable. It must mean that the Change was truly changing things all over again. But if someplace as idyllic as this could go plotless, could anyplace in the Cineverse be safe?

"Come now, my children!" the elder cautioned. "Our esteemed visitors did not come to our happy island to hear such negative things. Think about all the progress we have made of late."

"In what?" one of the other islanders yelled.

"Well, cooking, for one thing," the elder insisted. "We had not had much time to explore the culinary arts before, what with our full schedule of human sacrifices and what not. Now, though, a whole new field has opened before us."

The other islanders did not look at all enthusiastic.

"I am sure our visitors will agree with me," the elder continued defensively, "when they taste my Coconut Surprise!"

"But we have these outsiders here, now!" one of the maidens objected. "Surely, with them around, there must be a score of new plots!"

"Yes!" another agreed. "Perhaps we can get them, through their own ignorance, to profane a sacred island object!"

"Say," one of the men suggested, "why don't we have them toss litter into our sacred volcano?"

"Not only a tried and true theme," another added, "but also ecologically correct!"

"No, I have an even better idea!" yet another of the maidens interjected. "Why not have them all come in on a ship and discover us—"

"Yes! Yes!" one of the fellows added enthusiastically, caught up in the moment. "And they try to force us to shed our heathen ways and take up the trappings of civilization—"

"—and *then* they can profane the sacred volcano!" the maiden concluded. "What a plot!"

All the islanders, save the village elder, applauded.

Delores cleared her throat. "Well," she said. "Yes."

"Are you sure," the elder inquired, "while you're thinking about this, you wouldn't want to try one of my Coconut Kabobs?"

Delores phrased her answer carefully: "I'm afraid, as good as your plot sounds, and as tasty as those Coconut Kabobs must be, we have time for neither. We are here on a mission that affects not only this island paradise, but all of the Cineverse!"

"Really?" one of the islanders allowed. "That kind of plot doesn't sound half bad, either. And, incidentally, isn't that Dwight the Wonder Dog?"

"Bark, yip, bark!" Dwight agreed.

"Yes," Delores replied before Officer O'Clanrahan could butt in, "the dog everybody knows. As I was saying, we must scale the side of Wakka Loa, and find the last place we saw the Secret Samoan, also known as Captain Crusader. That way, Dwight can pick up the Captain's scent, and follow him anywhere in the Cineverse!"

"Actually," one of the locals pointed out, "the island doesn't have all that big a part in that, does it?"

"Yeah," another agreed. "I really like the well-meaning-encroachments-of-civilization-accidentally-offending-our-sacred-deities plot a lot better!''

But Delores was adamant. "I'm sorry, but it's my plot or none at all. We must find Captain Crusader. After all, the Cineverse is at stake.''

There were a few minutes of dejected barefoot scraping and grass-skirt rustling, but, in the end, the islanders agreed. The elder waved the others to silence.

"So it is that our delightful visitors choose to climb the monarch of our island in the sun, Wakka Loa. And who knows? Perhaps, when they feel it is time to take a rest, they will be in the mood for some of my Braised Coconut in White Wine Sauce?''

Delores thanked all the islanders, then turned to lead the way up the long and winding path to the pinnacle of the now dormant volcano, Wakka Loa. Everybody else on the island followed.

It seemed to take far longer to climb the steep slope than it had the last time she had done this. Of course, the last time, she had also been under the spell of the drums of the Volcano God. Minutes turned to hours as the sun raced across the sky overhead, and still they climbed. Once again, she could hear disgruntled mumblings among the islanders about how much more interesting it would be to use the profaned idol plot, along with the occasional suggestion from the village elder that perhaps everyone might like some Coconut Flambé.

But Delores knew they could not stop. The Cineverse was unraveling around her, and the more time it took for them to find Captain Crusader, the more difficult it might be to put it all back together. By the time they reached the sacrificial altars just beneath the summit, it was late afternoon, and the tropical sun hung halfway behind the towering cone of Wakka Loa, throwing a great black-on-black shadow across the pumice plane.

She couldn't see anything under that shadow. It was amazing, Delores thought, that there could be so little light while it was still afternoon. Perhaps her eyes had been dazzled by too much squinting in the tropical sun. Or perhaps, she thought, her worst fears once again surfacing, there was something else.

That's when Delores heard an all-too-familiar voice from the darkness.

"We have to stop meeting like this," the monster intoned.

⟁ 11 ⟁
"Sisters of Doom!"

Something was wrong here.

The blue smoke had cleared. Roger found himself on a stark, colorless plane, the almost featureless horizon before him broken only by a few scrawny, leafless trees which rattled in the chill wind. But it was even worse when he looked up into the equally colorless sky, for where there should have been clouds, there were other things.

A huge, blinking eye stared down at him as it rolled across the heavens, followed by a grandfather clock, ticking, ticking, ticking as its hands chased each other wildly about the dial. That, too, blew away, and a giant baby tumbled across the horizon, crying soundlessly in the air far overhead, its great, pudgy hands grasping for things it would never find.

Roger frowned. This place seemed to have even less connection with reality than the other worlds he had visited. Worse than that, all that stuff going on up in the sky looked suspiciously like—he hated to even think the word—symbolism.

Roger didn't have to wait for anyone to sing or speak here. He knew all too well where the Captain Crusader Decoder Ring had deposited him this time. Rampant symbolism of this sort could mean only one thing.

He was in an Art Film.

Roger told himself to stay calm. Perhaps, if he considered his surroundings and what was likely to happen here, he might even fare better than he had on other worlds in the Cineverse. He might actually manage some degree of control. In order to do that, however, he had to think. . . .

What exactly happened in an Art Film?

A lot of the time, not much—was the answer that came to mind. Depending on the specific film, people tended to drink a lot of coffee, or stare moodily out of windows for hours on end, or fall asleep and have visions that usually had something to do with their generally failed lives. That's what the things riding through the sky reminded Roger of— those hallucinatory yet super-real visions.

Was there anything else in these films? Roger thought back to the hundreds—maybe thousands—he had seen.

Mostly, Roger realized, in this kind of movie, they liked to talk.

"Smolny norma?"

Roger jumped. Someone had spoken in his ear. He whirled around to see a thin and haggard man dressed all in black. The man glanced blankly at Roger, the barest bit of curiosity underlying his misery, then let his gaze return to the fantastic sky, through which a troop of nuns were marching as they played on flutes and gongs.

"Smolny norma?" he asked again.

Roger started. He had been looking half at the man, half at the all-nun band. Still, he could have sworn that he saw something white flash near the man's worn, dark leather belt.

"Pardon?" Roger asked, pulling the haggard fellow's gaze away from the sky.

"Smolny norma!" the other man repeated heavily, his

disgust barely apparent beneath the almost overwhelming malaise.

Yes! Roger's heart jumped. It was definitely there. His mind leapt as well. This meant two things:

First, this fellow was not speaking English. Therefore, this was not only an Art Film. It was a Foreign Art Film.

But with that came the second realization, for when the haggard man had spoken, Roger had seen a white line appear across his waist—a line made up of letters. It was that line that had given Roger hope. For, even though he had found himself on a film world where they spoke some incomprehensible language, still Roger would be able to understand, because this world was subtitled!

Not, of course, that Roger had had a chance to read that subtitle. He had been too excited by the very existence of that line of letters to do any more than simply react. He looked again at the haggard fellow, who still stared moodily at the sky. Roger cleared his throat, but got no reaction. Perhaps, Roger thought with a bit of panic, he had missed his chance, and this gaunt fellow would never speak again.

Roger told himself to calm down. As he had already reminded himself, all they did in Art Films was talk. Not that they necessarily said anything—except through implication—but talking would be the major, and sometimes the only, action on a movie world of this type. It was so central to this sort of place that even the Change couldn't have affected it. Everybody *had* to talk.

In fact, Roger realized, maybe it was time he did some talking of his own. Roger stared at the air, a few feet in front of him and down a bit, parallel to his waist. He spoke:

"Smolny norma?"

What he saw next filled him simultaneously with delight and despair.

He did have his own subtitle. It hung, shimmering, in the air, just about where he guessed it would be, the letters clearly legible.

But not readable. The pattern of letters before him made
no sense.

?EREH UOY ERA YHW

At least, that's what he thought it said. Some of the letters
were positioned backwards as well. Were the subtitles in
yet another foreign tongue? If that was true, how could he
possibly understand anything?

Wait a moment. Backwards letters? What if you turned
those letters around? What if you turned the whole sentence
around? Roger did some quick mental shuffling.

HERE . . . YOU . . . ARE . . . WHY.

WHY ARE YOU HERE?

Of course! Now that he thought of it, it only made sense
that the subtitle was backwards. Before this, he had always
read these words sitting in a movie theater, looking up at
a screen. Back then, he had been an outsider looking in.
Now, however, in this Art Film corner of the Cineverse,
he had become part of the movie. Therefore the subtitle *had*
to be backwards!

Roger chuckled. Why are you here? He clapped his hands.
It was so simple!

He stopped when he saw the haggard man glaring at him.
Behind him, white swans flew in a circular formation in a
storm-cloud heavy sky.

"Smolny norma?" the other man repeated.

His subtitle was the same. ?EREH UOY ERA YHW—still
backwards. Roger found it a bit disconcerting, but he supposed it made sense, insofar as anything made sense on a
Foreign Art Film world.

The haggard man did not wait for a reply, but spoke
again.

"Smolny ava?"

Roger quickly scanned the subtitle:

?EREH I MA YHW

It took Roger only a second to reverse this one:

WHY AM I HERE?

Roger nodded. Yes, he guessed that was what he had

asked. He'd have to be careful when he tried to speak in a foreign language. He wouldn't want to be misunderstood.

"Smolny stephanie!" the haggard man demanded. Roger quickly read the subtitle that followed.

?EREH YDOBYNA SI YHW

WHY IS ANYBODY HERE?

Had there been any doubts about the true nature of this place in which Roger now found himself, that last answer would have swept them away. How existential could this environment get?

The haggard man walked stiff-legged past Roger. He never did seem to wait for an answer. In the sky, a fat man was picking lint from his belly button.

Roger turned his head to follow the haggard fellow's progress and was startled to see a building of some sort only a few yards distant. Had the fantastic sky so unsettled him that he had completely neglected to register his surroundings? Roger decided to believe that, rather then the alternative—that the countryside might be every bit as unpredictable as the sky overhead.

He hurried to follow the haggard fellow, which really wasn't all that difficult. The other man shuffled along very slowly, as if he didn't particularly want to get anywhere. Roger had to slow his pace so he wouldn't pass his haggard companion. He used the extra time to examine the building they had almost reached.

The place had fallen into disrepair. Chunks of bone-white plaster littered the walk before them. One of the two windows on this side of the structure was smashed. Between the bits of shattered glass, Roger could see a spider web that glistened in the strange, autumnal light.

As they rounded the corner, Roger saw what must have once been a steeple, rising above the building's roof. He realized this derelict shell before them had at one time served as a church for some austere religious sect. The haggard man came to a doorway, one rusted hinge the only testimony that this space had previously held a door. He staggered inside. Roger followed.

The church was in as sorry a state within as it had been outside. A woman, also dressed in black, sat in the midst of the half dozen broken pews that still remained. She looked up as the two men entered. The expression on her face made the haggard man appear cheerful.

"Smolny valarie?" she demanded.

WHY IS HE HERE? the subtitle read. Roger thought that, thus far, the level of conversation in this place left something to be desired.

The haggard man, ignoring her question, asked her one in turn.

"Minsky shirley gevornen?"

WHERE IS YOUR SISTER?

The woman jerked back violently, as though she had been slapped. She looked about as if suspicious of eavesdroppers, her eyes flicking back and forth like scurrying beetles. When she spoke again, it was in a whisper:

"Morden vorden gehunden."

SHE IS LOOKING FOR HER DOG.

Roger concentrated, trying to detect key words or patterns in their conversation. Somehow, he had to communicate with these people.

The haggard man glanced distractedly at a rat that scurried between the broken pews. His reply was more full of anguish than anything he had said before.

"Katrina. Nurden varden stubben?"

KATRINA. WHY DO YOU PERSIST?

But Katrina only smiled at that. Her eyes stopped their beetle-dance and became slightly unfocused, as if she were looking far beyond the church. She spoke at last, her voice a happy singsong:

"Storg! Piers, gnurden vurd volley-volley expresso."

The subtitle was longer this time:

I MUST. PIERS, YOU CAN SEE HER BREATH RISE IN SMALL CLOUDS BEYOND THE HILLS.

Piers only shook his head.

"Smeltzny heloise?" he demanded.

WHERE CAN SHE BE?

Roger could not let this go on forever. He had given up trying to make any exact sense out of their conversation, but he believed he might have identified a few key words and phrases. They had said enough now so that he might even be able to ask a simple question, so long as he kept his vocabulary as basic as possible. Silently he formed the question in English: "I must see Captain Crusader. Where is he?" It was simple enough. Surely, even though the words might not be in the right order, the sense of his question should get through.

He coughed rather loudly. Both Piers and Katrina turned to look at him.

Roger spoke quickly:

"Storg gnurden Captain Crusader. Minsky smeltzny valarie?"

Both Piers and Katrina stared at him, open-mouthed.

This was not quite the reaction Roger had been hoping for. His eyes slid down to the subtitle before him:

YOUR SISTER HAS DOG BREATH. AM I CAPTAIN CRUSADER?

Piers turned to Katrina. Roger was too upset to listen to what the haggard man was saying. He couldn't help himself, though. He had to read the subtitle.

HE HAS MET YOUR SISTER.

Katrina's reply was angry. Once again, Roger didn't really listen, but only read:

I HAVE NO CONTROL OVER HER PERSONAL HYGIENE.

But then Katrina turned to Roger and smiled. The expression changed her face. Her whole countenance opened up, and the years fell away. Sunlight seemed to be reflected in her eyes. Roger realized that, before this misery descended upon her, she had been rather pretty.

"Blorfen," she urged. "Inka minka mensky smelten."

COME, the subtitle explained. I WILL TAKE YOU TO MY SISTER.

Roger nodded, a gesture she seemed to understand. He was glad Katrina had forgiven him for his first blundering attempt at their language. Perhaps, given a little more time, he might find some way of communicating with this pair. He had to, if he was to discover where he was, and where he should go in his search for Captain Crusader. The computer, after all, had programmed his ring to lead him to the Captain's most likely whereabouts—perhaps not this bleakly symbolic place, but certainly a world nearby.

Katrina rose from her pew. She fussed with her hair in a broken shard of mirror that she pulled from a worn leather bag. She seemed so much happier than before.

Roger felt a heavy hand on his shoulder. He turned to see the frightened face of Piers.

"Mensky valarie," he whispered urgently. "Urken blurgeon gesundheit."

Roger's heart almost stopped when he read the subtitle: HER SISTER HAS BEEN DEAD FOR A LONG TIME.

Piers nodded when he saw Roger's concern. He made a slashing motion across his throat, the sort of gesture that meant the same thing in any language.

Roger swallowed sharply as Piers faded back into the shadows.

Katrina hummed happily to herself as she put her mirror away. She fingered something at her belt—something black that looked like the hilt of an object whose hidden part would be very sharp indeed.

"Blorfen," she told Roger. "Sharpen slashen kooten!"

COME, the subtitle reassured. YOU WILL JOIN HER SHORTLY.

She reached out to take his hand, presumably to lead him to his death. Her other hand still held onto the black hilt. Roger glanced behind him, but Piers seemed to have disappeared.

For a second, Roger felt there was no escape.

But he wasn't trapped. He had his Captain Crusader Secret Decoder Ring. So what if he didn't know where he was? So what if he didn't have the slightest clue to the whereabouts of Captain Crusader? If he stuck around here, there was a good chance he would very shortly be dead.

He pulled the ring from his pocket and twisted it violently.

"See you in the funny papers!"

Nothing happened. The ring didn't work.

Only then did Roger realize how foolish he had been. This ring hadn't been designed to help him find Captain Crusader. Far from it. This ring had been made by the renegade computer VERA, a machine programmed by the minions of Doctor Dread, no doubt to strand him somewhere far away from Captain Crusader, a spot on the most distant edge of the Cineverse, from which he could never return. By using this ring at the Institute of Very Advanced Science, he hadn't escaped Dread's plans; he had played right into his hands!

Katrina grabbed his wrist. For one so frail, she was surprisingly strong. She dragged him from the church in a matter of seconds.

"Minsky mensky smertzen bludengutsen!" she cried passionately.

MY SISTER WILL BE SO GLAD TO HAVE COMPANY, the subtitle read.

Katrina yanked the blade from her sash.

"Gerenden undsmashen!" she screamed. "Chopen hacken slashen gooshen!"

Roger didn't read the subtitle. All he could see was the knife.

⟨ 12 ⟩
"Deadly Coincidence!"

"Cripes!" Big Louie exclaimed. "Is this guy everywhere?"

Delores managed to nod. She had difficulty even moving her head. She had begun to think of this whole thing as inevitable. The Slime Monster was omnipresent. He was one with shadow—every shadow. Wherever there was darkness, there was slime.

"Good," the monster remarked from somewhere within the lightlessness before her. "It will be so much easier, once you surrender to the inevitable."

Delores didn't know what to say. Instead, she shivered violently in the island heat.

"So few people have taken the time to get to know me," the monster remarked. "They don't understand the purpose of my slime."

"Purpose?" Zabana demanded. "Slime not have purpose. Slime is slime!"

"See?" The monster sighed. "It has been that way throughout the Cineverse. But with Delores by my side, I know it would be different."

121

Delores tried to get control of herself. She had never actually seen this monster, after all. Perhaps it wasn't as bad as she imagined. Shivering in broad daylight, jumping at the approach of shadows—this was no way for a hero to act! She was tumbling into some kind of slime-induced shock.

No, she couldn't let her revulsion control her life. She had to approach this whole thing dispassionately, like she had been taught in Hero School, especially in Narrow Escapes 301. After all, what would life be like with a slime monster?

She envisioned an existence surrounded by slippery goo; swimming in a lake of viscous mush. She imagined it would all be rather like living in a mucous membrane. Her stomach lurched as bile rose in her throat. She wished, as soon as she had thought of it, that she could forget that analogy.

That's when Officer O'Clanrahan stepped between Delores and the shadow.

"I'm sorry, boyo!" the policeman interjected. "It's soundin' to me like you want to put this little lady in jeopardy. And where there are women in jeopardy, where there are wrongs to be righted, where there are dangers to be overcome—that's where you'll find Dwight the Wonder Dog!"

"Bark, yip, arf!" Dwight agreed.

"Dwight would like to remind you, even though you lurk in darkness," Louie explained, "that Wonder Dogs have exceptional night vision."

"Yip, bark, arf!" Dwight emphasized.

"But you misunderstand me," the voice replied softly. "Monsters are always misunderstood."

Zabana nodded his head in agreement. "Is Law of Cineverse!"

"Exactly," the slime creature agreed. "Delores has nothing to fear from me. I do not want to destroy. I want to create!"

Create? Delores started to shiver all over again.

"Wait a second, here, missy," Doc reassured her coolly.

"This slime fella has a slippery tongue. I think my years as a crusading frontier lawyer might come in handy here. Would you mind, Mr. Slime, if I asked you a few questions?"

"My friends call me Edward," the monster replied.

"Edward?" Doc asked in surprise.

"Exactly," the monster answered darkly. "Not Ed, and never, ever Eddie. Edward."

"Well, Edward," Doc continued smoothly, "we here are all friends of Delores, so, naturally, we are concerned for her welfare."

"I would never harm her welfare," the monster insisted.

"Certainly not," Doc hastily agreed. "But I'm afraid we worry about other parts of her as well."

Delores forcibly shook herself. This was ridiculous. She was ignoring a prime tenet of Hero School, and—rather than acting—allowing herself to be acted upon. She had to force her imagination to stop running in its unpleasantly squishy direction, and stand up to this thing.

"What if I don't want to go with you?" she demanded.

The monster's answer was the epitome of calm:

"Then I will wait."

"Wait?" She laughed, her anger rising now that she had found her voice. "You'll have to wait an awfully long time!"

"Perhaps," Edward the monster allowed. "Sooner or later, you will come to me."

Officer O'Clanrahan allowed his hand to rest meaningfully on the nightstick at his belt. "You're awfully sure of yourself, boyo!"

"Eventually, all is slime," was the monster's only reply.

"I hate to break into this cross-examination," Louie said, "but don't we have a Cineverse to save?"

"It is true!" the village elder added helpfully. "Our visitors, along with an unspeakable something hiding in the shadows, have reached the pinnacle of Wakka Loa, a tourist highlight of our island paradise! The unparalleled view of the ocean from this great height is truly breathtaking, as our guests search for—''

"Hey, dad," one of the islanders interrupted. "Don't rush things here, huh? This is the most interesting plot we've had on this island since I can't remember when!"

"Save the Cineverse?" the monster asked. "I did not realize you were on a mission."

"Of course not!" Officer O'Clanrahan exclaimed between gritted teeth. "All you were concerned with was your inhuman lust!"

"Inhuman lust?" Edward repeated, horrified. "No, it's much more aesthetic than that. Oh, why must we monsters be misunderstood?"

"Is Law of Cineverse," Zabana repeated.

"Well, wait a second here," Doc clarified. "Do you mean that, since we are on a mission to save the Cineverse, you will give up your pursuit of Delores and let us go on our way?"

"No," the monster answered, "Delores is still mine. But perhaps I will come along."

Somehow, Delores did not feel all that reassured by this turn of events.

"Yip! Arf arf! Bark!" Dwight added.

"Dwight says it's high time he got to sniffing out the last known whereabouts of Captain Crusader," Louie translated.

The others quickly agreed, and followed Dwight around the final bend to the pumice plateau where Delores and all her friends had almost been sacrificed not so long ago. There, in front of her, were the three tables where she and the others were to be strapped. Her throat felt dry as she looked at the nearest of the altars, that stone tablet table-top equipped with a central drain hole to dispense with any extra blood—blood that would then run straight down through crevices in the mountain, right to the heart of the thirsty volcano!

"Bark! Yip yip! Arf!" Dwight announced.

"He asks that you all step back and give him room,"

Louie illuminated. "He has to pick up Captain Crusader's scent."

Everyone quickly moved to the perimeter of the plateau as Dwight put his nose to the ground and began to sniff.

A couple of the islanders, one male, one female, sidled back over to the Slime Monster's shadow.

"Are you sure we couldn't convince you to stick around?" the fellow asked the lightless space.

"Yeah!" the woman added. "You're the best plot device we've seen in ages!"

"Sorry—" the monster began.

"We'd let you menace our women for hours," the man promised.

"Of course," the woman remarked regretfully, "you'd have to be sacrificed to our Volcano God eventually—"

"But we promise we'd make it worth your while!" the man concluded.

"I apologize again, but it is impossible," Edward replied firmly. "For a long time, ever since I can remember, I have thought that slime was my destiny. Now, however, I know differently. My destiny is slime, and Delores."

"Yip, bark bark, yip!" Dwight declared excitedly. His tail wagged energetically as he danced around a spot behind the sacrificial tables.

There, wedged in a crack in the hardened lava, was a single, small bongo drum—one of the drums that Captain Crusader, in his guise as the Secret Samoan, had used to communicate with Wakka Loa!

"So this was the last place Captain Crusader was on our world?" Delores asked.

"Yip yip!" Dwight agreed.

"And you can follow him to the next world he visited?" Delores added.

"Bark bark!" Dwight assured her.

"Well, what are we waiting for?" Louie asked. "Let's go Captain-hunting!"

"Very good." Delores waved to the others to gather round. "It's time to travel."

"I will follow, in my own way," the Slime Monster declared from somewhere in his shadow.

Delores decided she had to ignore the amorous creature's intentions. They had to locate Captain Crusader and save the Cineverse. Any personal considerations would have to wait until all the cosmic perils were dealt with. But she had a more immediate problem.

"How do we set the ring?" Delores asked with a frown.

"Bark bark. Yip, bark!" Dwight replied.

"You'll have to hand him the ring," Louie explained with a nod to the canine. "The Wonder Dog will hold it in his teeth and turn it with his tongue."

Delores did as she was asked as her companions gathered around her to form a human chain. Louie hooked a hand around the Wonder Dog's collar.

"And so, once again, our visitors reluctantly leave our island paradise—" the village elder began.

"That's it?" one of the islanders demanded.

Others picked up on his anger.

"You're just going to let them go?" another added.

"You're the village elder!" one of the lovely young maidens reminded him. "Aren't you going to do anything?"

"Oh, yes," the elder hastily added. "I see what you mean." He turned to Delores and her noble band. "Pardon me. Would you like some Coconut Krispies for the trip?"

"No!" the first islander wailed. "We are doomed to a life of plotlessness!"

"Now, now, it's not as bad as all that," the elder counseled. "Maybe—um—we could get them to quickly profane something before they leave. That sort of thing really only takes a minute, after all, and we could pretend the volcano wasn't quite so dormant—"

"I'm sorry," Delores said with finality, "but we really must be going."

Dwight wagged his tail agitatedly. He looked like he

wanted to say something but couldn't with the ring held between his teeth.

"So we're trapped," the first islander replied glumly.

"Wait!" one of the maidens objected. "Why can't they take us with them?"

"Sure," another of the islanders added. "Then they could profane something at their leisure!"

"Not a bad idea," the elder admitted. "If we, upon our island paradise, are out of plots, why not travel to those far distant lands where we might find some more?"

But Delores shook her head firmly. "It cannot be done. As much as we would like to help, we cannot bring you along. I am transporting so many already with a single Captain Crusader Decoder Ring, I'm afraid we would overload if we added any more." She glanced down at the dull silver ring in her hand. "It may be the key to the universe, but it's only made out of cheap plastic, after all."

"Don't you worry none, fellas," Doc reassured the islanders. "Your island is not the only place that's suffered 'cause of Doctor Dread. Things have changed in the Cineverse, but our mission is to change them back, or to make them even better than before! Jumpin' Jehoshaphat! Before long, you'll have too many plots to even think!"

"Very well," the elder replied with a sigh, resigned to his fate. "So our contented visitors leave this happy isle, refusing to take so much as a Coconut Upside Down Cake along for their—"

"See you in the funny papers!" Delores yelled. The blue smoke took them away.

"Yip, yip, yip! Bark, arf!" Dwight started in before the smoke had a chance to clear. Delores found the Captain Crusader Decoder Ring—now a little wetter than before— back in her hand.

"We're getting close!" Louie explained. "The heroic scent is particularly strong. Captain Crusader has spent a lot of time here!"

Delores tensed. She always had this trouble when she was stuck in this thick blue smoke. The lack of visibility alone couldn't help but make one apprehensive. Where exactly was *here*? If it was someplace where Captain Crusader spent a lot of time—where he was particularly needed—it might be even more dangerous than all the other places they had already visited.

And that brought up another question she hadn't had time to ask herself: What would they do if they actually found Captain Crusader? So much had happened in the last few days that they really had had no time to plan a definite course of action—or even to ask some of the obvious questions that arose from this situation. The Change seemed to be speeding up. Whatever the exact nature of Doctor Dread's sinister plans, they seemed to be working. Shouldn't Captain Crusader, by his very nature, be aware of this? Shouldn't he already be fighting the good fight without being sought out and asked to help? What if he had fallen under some world's spell, like Doctor Dread in Bunnyland? What if Captain Crusader was missing because of some secret that only the hero among heroes was privy to?

What if—Delores thought with a cold suddenness—what if Captain Crusader knew where she could find Roger? With all their recent battles and narrow escapes, she had tried to push the man from Earth out of her mind. But Roger meant more to her than she had ever dared admit. She had to find him somehow—anyhow. But how could she?—if to search for Roger, she had to ignore the very destiny of the Cineverse.

Delores shook her head. There were no answers. Better to concentrate on this new world, and the clues to Captain Crusader's whereabouts.

She heard the sound of the ocean. Had they never left the South Sea Island Paradise? But no, there were any number of Cineverse worlds where the sea played an important role. Perhaps, when the smoke cleared, they would find themselves on a pirate galleon, or on some huge luxury liner, a Grand Hotel of the seas. But there was another sound here, besides the breaking waves—a musical sound. Delores frowned. Was it an electric guitar?

The smoke blew away. They were on a beach somewhere, full of bright sand and sun, surrounded by men and women, most of them in bathing suits that had been out of style for twenty years.

"Hey!" one of the men yelled. "You're not Roger!"

Roger? Delores was speechless. Her Roger? Well, how many Rogers were likely to show up in the middle of a cloud of blue smoke? Could it be? She remembered how, only a moment ago, she hadn't wanted to think about him, she was so sure he must be dead. Either that, or he had been trapped back on Earth, unable to reach Delores or the Cineverse ever again!

But this changed everything! If he had come to this ocean-side world, that meant that he was not only alive, but had found some other means of traveling around the Cineverse!

One of the other men, a large, hulking fellow dressed in black leather, mumbled something sinister. He held something in his hand that looked like a switchblade.

"No, we are not Roger," Delores said, hoping to defuse any particularly difficult situations. "But we are friends of Roger."

The mumbling man put away his knife. Delores breathed a sigh of relief.

He picked up a tire iron instead. He mumbled something to the group of toughs immediately behind him. They reached into pockets, pulling out chains, brass knuckles, and two-by-four planks. Delores was amazed by the size of their pockets.

"Wait a minute!" she called to the assembled leather-suited gang. "We don't need to fight!"

The gang all laughed at that.

"If we have to fight, missy," Doc drawled, "we fight.

Least it's somethin' we know. There's worse things in the Cineverse.''

The gang started towards them.

"Hey, Bix!" one of the bathing-suited fellows called. "Don't you think it's time for a song?"

⪦ 13 ⪧

"Even More Flaming Death!"

"Slashen kooten blooden gooshen!" Katrina demanded.

It was only when Roger forced open one eye that he realized he had had them both closed. Katrina smiled at him.

In one hand she held the knife.

In the other hand she held the cheese.

Roger glanced down at the words that hovered around her waist.

YOU SHOULD EAT, the subtitle read. WE HAVE A LONG WALK AHEAD OF US.

It was a large slab of yellow cheese, with small holes, and an aged, crumbly texture.

"Slashen?" Roger repeated.

YOU SHOULD EAT, read his subtitle.

She nodded, cutting into the cheese.

"Kooten gooshen?" he added.

A LONG WALK AHEAD, the letters read this time.

Roger almost laughed. He had completely misunderstood the import of Katrina's speech. He had imagined, foolishly,

131

that whatever language she was speaking had some similarities to English. He should be careful, especially on a world burdened by rampant symbolism, in making any assumptions at all.

He accepted a slab of cheese. Katrina reached within the folds of her dress and retrieved a half-filled bottle of red wine. Roger uncorked it and took a swig. That was a problem with gallivanting around the Cineverse—you never had time to eat. It was only now that he realized how hungry he was.

Katrina walked a few paces down the worn path to a stone bench at the far corner of the church. She sat, and Roger followed, sitting at the bench's other end. He accepted another piece of cheese, and another swig of wine.

"Valerie smertzen gnoogen splooshna!" Katrina remarked as she cut another piece for herself.

Roger glanced over at the subtitle:

MY SISTER LIVES BY A LAKE.

Roger frowned. The cheese went down hard as he swallowed. But she had definitely said "lives," and not "died." Perhaps he had somehow misunderstood what Piers had been trying to tell him. Heaven knew, he could have run afoul of some colloquial idiom in the local language. Who knew how precise these subtitles were, anyway? Roger had already misinterpreted Katrina's actions once. Now, sitting with her on this bench, sharing cheese and wine, she couldn't look more unthreatening.

Roger looked up in the sky. There didn't seem to be any symbolism at all up there on this side of the church, only an endless expanse of white. It was true, Roger admitted: that endless sky could be considered bleak. But, with a full stomach and a proper frame of mind, it could also be considered peaceful.

Dr. Dee Dee Davenport had called him "incredibly lucky," and he supposed that he was. After all, he had visited maybe a dozen worlds in the Cineverse, many of them fraught with peril, and had escaped every one without a scratch. Maybe, Roger considered as he chewed, it was also a stroke of good fortune that had brought him to this Art Film world. This was the first place he'd been in the Cineverse where he could really pause and think.

He thought for an instant about the stranger with the blue-smoke cigar—the Plotmaster. He wondered if that mysterious figure had anything to do with his arriving in a contemplative place like this—if, indeed, he was being manipulated by this strange figure—manipulated along with everyone else in the Cineverse.

But too much contemplation, without facts to back it up, got Roger nowhere. No matter what the Plotmaster's plans were, Roger had to act for himself. He couldn't stay here, no matter how peaceful it seemed at the moment. He had to find Captain Crusader, save the Cineverse, figure out the riddle of the Plotmaster—and rescue Delores, if Delores was still rescuable. And that was just for starters.

A few minutes ago, his Captain Crusader Decoder Ring had failed to work, and he had panicked, blaming the failure on Professor Peril's tampering with the computer at the Institute of Very Advanced Science. But, now that he thought about it, there could be other reasons for that failure. What if there wasn't something wrong with the ring itself, but in the way he had used it? He was in a different place, with different rules, and a different language. What if—for the ring to work—he had to say "See you in the funny papers" in the native tongue?

Of course! It only made sense; at least as much sense as Professor Peril having enough foresight to get the computer to sabotage his ring. Maybe he could get off this world after all!

But how could he learn to say "See you in the funny papers" in the local lingo? Roger thought back to other movies he had seen, and how people who didn't speak the same language managed to communicate. They somehow managed to act out their wishes, didn't they? He glanced at Katrina, and she looked curiously back at him. Roger would somehow have to reach her through sign language.

He pointed to himself. "Roger," he said.

Katrina pointed to herself and repeated her name. So she had the idea!

Roger pointed to his eyes and said the first word he needed a translation for:

"See."

Katrina pointed to her own eye and said "Snortz!"

Roger eagerly looked at the subtitle.

EYE, it read.

Roger sighed. This wasn't going to be easy. He had to be more demonstrative. He placed his index finger along his temple. He first pointed to his eye, then shot the finger straight ahead, as if it were a ray of light.

"Ah!" Katrina replied in sudden comprehension. "Gleeba snortz!"

POINTING NEXT TO YOUR EYE, the translation read.

Roger wished he had played more charades in his life. How could you come up with sign language for one of the senses? You see with the eye. What could be simpler? Surely, in a world so fraught with symbolism, Katrina was bound to make the connection. He shook his head and repeated the index finger move.

"Ah!" Katrina gave a how-could-she-be-so-stupid chuckle. She added triumphantly: "Snortz felten zubba-zubba!"

That sounded a little long to be "see," but perhaps it was colloquial. Roger looked hopefully at the subtitle.

RIPPING YOUR EYE OUT AND THROWING IT A GREAT DISTANCE.

No. There had to be some other way to get his message across. Roger also didn't like the violent subtext of Katrina's suggestion. He thought again about Piers's fearful remarks concerning the dead sister.

But Roger couldn't give in to despair. He had Katrina working with him; he simply had to come up with a new approach. How did you indicate the senses? It was hard with the eyes.

Roger pointed to his nose.

"Smortz," Katrina replied.

NOSE, the subtitle read.

Roger sniffed exaggeratedly.

"Smortzen?" Katrina asked.

SMELL? was the subtitle. Yes! Roger was on the right track. He pointed back to his eye.

"Snortz?" Katrina ventured. "Snortzen?"

EYE? read the letters near her waist. SEE?

Yes! Roger nodded his head rapidly and clapped his hands. They were on their way! Katrina picked up right away on "me" and "you" when Roger pointed to both of them repeatedly. You was "norma"—he should have remembered that. Roger mimed laughter, and got the word "snucksky" from Katrina. But how was he going to come up with the word for papers?

That's when he remembered the book he'd stuck inside his elastic waistband: *The Cineverse—From A to Zed*. He'd simply point at one page, then another.

PAMPHLET, came the subtitled response. Then PERIODI-CAL. Then POINTING. Roger crinkled a corner of the page.

"Storken," Katrina replied.

PAPER, the subtitle read.

Roger nodded, crumpling a second page.

"Storkena?" Katrina added.

"Yes!" Roger shouted.

"Snucksen vorden merkna valarie," Katrina announced.

I AM GLAD YOU ARE SO HAPPY. HOWEVER, WE MUST SEE MY SISTER BEFORE DARK. SHE IS EXPECTING US, AFTER ALL, AND THE DISTANCE, WHILE NOT GREAT, CAN BE TIRING, ESPECIALLY IF YOU HAVE TO WALK INTO THE WIND.

Katrina had said all that? There was obviously a lot about this language that Roger had yet to figure out.

Roger stood up and pointed down the path.

"Go?" he inquired.

"Oucsh!" she exclaimed as she also stood. "Minsky vlerben mordet karben tertra koriden zumma-zumma nigs-

lipzen bedorm valarie krensk niebelungenkameradshaften-
volkswagen shaboom shaboom!"

YES was the only word that appeared at her waist. Then
again, Roger realized, there might be some problems with
the translation.

Katrina led the way at a brisk pace. Roger hurried to
keep up, but somehow she managed to stay a good dozen
feet in front of him. He pulled out his ring. He had the
translation for "See you in the funny papers." He might
as well see if it would work. Was there any last thing he
wanted to say to his guide?

"Katrina!" he called.

"Glorben snurbs!" she shouted back without looking
around. And this time there was no subtitle at all.

Very well. There was probably no need for explanations
if he disappeared from a place like this. The locals would
simply chalk it up to more symbolism.

He took a deep breath and twisted the ring.

"Snortzen stephanie snucksky storkena!" he yelled.

Nothing happened. He looked at the subtitle.

LOOKING AT YOU WITH THE HUMOROUS BOOKS!

Well, that might not have been exactly what he wanted,
but it should have been close enough, shouldn't it? Then,
why had nothing happened? Maybe he hadn't spoken with
enough conviction.

He said the foreign phrase again, slowly and clearly,
twisting the ring the other way.

"Snortzen stephanie snucksky storkena!"

Still nothing but the same subtitle about looking at humorous books. And if that phrase wasn't close enough, he
didn't know how he could get any closer. Maybe the Professor Peril theory was right after all.

Katrina glanced over her shoulder without slackening her
pace. "Minsky mensky geslunden?" she demanded. She
didn't have any subtitle this time either.

Wait a second, Roger realized. Wasn't there some flick-
ering against the sky? Why hadn't he seen this before? It

wasn't as if this were anything new—he always had this sort of problem with foreign films. With Katrina so far ahead of him, the letters must be appearing all the way on the other side of her, right up against that colorless sky, making the subtitles white on white and completely illegible.

So her words were lost to him. Roger hoped whatever she had said wasn't essential to the plot. Although, now that he thought about it, what did the plot matter if he couldn't use his Captain Crusader Decoder Ring?

He followed Katrina listlessly to the lake, which—despite her protestations of hardship and distance—was only over the next hill. The water showed the same lack of color as the sky, and the modest expanse of liquid was bordered only by a few more of those ever-present barren trees, and a small shack, which, if Roger had been feeling more generous than his present circumstances allowed, he might have classified as a hovel.

Katrina walked straight to the shack. She banged on the door.

"Valarie zurben-zurben," she told Roger authoritatively.

MY SISTER WILL ANSWER.

The subtitle, appearing against the dark and rotting wood, was once again legible. Katrina banged on the door again. There was no sound from inside.

Katrina frowned at Roger.

"Glurben knocken kneesa."

YOU SEEM NERVOUS.

Roger jumped at the suggestion. "Uh—" he faltered. But how could he explain when he didn't know the language?

"Smeltzny Piers geblurben?" she demanded.

WHAT DID PIERS TELL YOU ABOUT MY SISTER?

What use was it to lie? Roger—after a second's thought to consider the most appropriate pantomime—clutched his heart and fell to the ground. Katrina began to speak rapidly. Roger pushed himself to his knees so that he could read the subtitle.

THAT SHE WAS DEAD? DO NOT BELIEVE HIM. MY SISTER LIV IS QUITE ALIVE. IT IS PIERS WHO CANNOT ACCEPT THE TRUTH.

Accepting the truth? This was sounding more like an Art Film with every passing minute. What was the truth? And should Roger even care?

He stumbled to his feet. He almost fell over again when the shack's door flew open.

"Gretzky!" Katrina said triumphantly. "Birdenparish."

SEE? the subtitle read. LIV IS ALIVE.

Her sister rushed from the shack. Her hair was a matted gray tangle that flopped about her head, her eyes two blazing points of blue in an unnaturally pale face, her clothing little more than tattered rags hanging from her emaciated body.

Her hands grabbed Roger's neck in a stranglehold.

"Viola canseco wadeboggs," Katrina confided.

SHE IS ALSO QUITE MAD Roger read with his blurring vision.

"Lars," Katrina's sister whispered hoarsely.

LARS her subtitle read. Roger tried, ineffectually, to pry her iron fingers from his throat. Katrina said something in return, but the sound of pounding blood was too loud on Roger's ears for him to catch the words. He could, however, just barely read the subtitle:

YES. I HAVE BROUGHT YOU LARS, AND I HAVE BROUGHT YOU A KNIFE. IT'S ALMOST BRAND NEW, ONLY USED TO CUT CHEESE.

Lars? Knife? Roger struggled to comprehend. The mad Liv eased her hold for an instant, and Roger tried to think of something, anything, he could say to make her stop. He hadn't figured out all that many of the words, and now he couldn't remember any of them. Still, he knew he had to try, if he didn't want to die. Maybe the very sound of his voice would disturb the mad sister enough so that he might break away.

"Mensky—uh—valarie—gesundheit—uh—*urk*!"

The last sound came as Liv once again tightened her grip.

COME TO ME, the subtitle read, MY LITTLE PIGLET.

How could he have said anything like that? The pressure increased at his throat. Roger was almost too upset to struggle. He didn't even know the word for piglet! Katrina was talking to her sister again. He managed to read the subtitle:

KILL THIS ONE SLOWLY, WOULD YOU? IT IS SO STRESSFUL TO FIND REPLACEMENTS.

Liv nodded and shook Roger by the throat one more time. He said *Urk* again for good measure.

PIGLET, the subtitle read. Liv kicked him in the kneecap.

Katrina smiled at Roger and said a final few words just for him:

IT IS NOT MUCH, BUT IT KEEPS HER HAPPY.

She turned to go, and Liv yanked Roger inside by the throat. She threw him down on a corner pile of straw. His head hit something hard. He gasped for breath, but it was no use. Liv's grip had been too firm, the knock on the back of his head too solid. The oddly spaced boards that crisscrossed the hovel's roof swirled wildly overhead.

He could feel his consciousness slipping . . .

slipping . . .

slipping . . .

slipping. . . .

He struggled to stay awake, but the world swung around him at a fantastic speed, colors bleeding, objects blurring . . .

blurring . . .

blurring . . .

blurring. . . .

Was there an echo in here somewhere?

And, for that matter, where was "here" anyway?

He wasn't in the hovel anymore. The colors around here were much too bright. He squinted, trying to bring the passing objects into focus.

Something large and pink and pudgy was screaming in the distance—actually, caterwauling would be a better description—a great booming cry like—Roger realized—a giant baby.

Another sound overlay the baby's cries, a steady, rhythmic sound. Roger turned around. His surroundings were becoming clearer. It was much easier to make out the clock face with the twirling hands.

Tick tock, went the clock.

Tick tock . . .

   Tick tock . . .

      Tick tock . . .

Yes, there was a definite echo around here. He heard another sound as the ticking faded, a mix of flutes and drums. Roger didn't have to turn around to know it was the all-nun band. He realized what all this meant. He had been wrong when he thought he had gone to some new world.

He was still in the Art Film, only more so.

He had fallen into a dream sequence.

A voice boomed over him, a voice that came from infinity:

BRAVO!

"Pardon?" Roger replied. He had heard that voice before. It surprised him not at all that he was turning around without using any of his muscles—this was a dream sequence, after all—nor did it surprise him that he was now facing the man with the blue-smoke cigar.

ROGER, SWEETIE, BABY!

The man's voice boomed again as he waved his cigar. It was the Plotmaster in silhouette, backlit as usual, so that Roger couldn't make out any of the finer details of the man's appearance. Somewhere, faintly, in the distance, Roger could hear a heavenly chorus—a Mormon Tabernacle Choir sort of sound.

Roger could still tell the Plotmaster was studying him critically.

NOT SURPRISED AT ALL

the Plotmaster said at last, then took a puff on his cigar.
Blue smoke curled upwards, encircling the all-nun band who
marched upside-down above his head. The choir music was
lost for a moment beneath the clatter of drums and the
tooting of flutes.

SO YOU *DO* REMEMBER ME?
AND YOU'VE ACCURATELY IDENTIFIED YOUR SURROUNDINGS!

Oh, dear, Roger thought. He wasn't supposed to remember this fellow, was he? He hoped the Plotmaster didn't
hold a grudge. Now that Roger considered it, the dark silhouette of a man smoking a cigar could appear rather threatening.

"I'm afraid I do—remember you, that is," Roger replied
softly. "Is this a problem?"

But the Plotmaster laughed.

PROBLEM?
I LIKE TO THINK OF IT MORE AS A PLOT COMPLICATION.
AND, HEY!
I *LIKE* TO USE PLOT COMPLICATIONS.
THEY DON'T CALL ME THE PLOTMASTER FOR NOTHING, BOOBALA!

Roger guessed he should be relieved. But this was all so
strange—

The Plotmaster snapped his fingers.

OF COURSE, I COULD CANCEL YOUR CONTRACT JUST LIKE *THAT*!

Snap . . .
    Snap . . .

Snap . . .
    Snap . . .
        Snap . . .

There was that echo again. Cancel his contract? Did that
mean what Roger thought it meant?

The Plotmaster pointed his cigar at Roger. The ember on
the stogie's end burned blue.

I'M THE BIG GUY AROUND HERE.
NEVER FORGET THAT.
AND IF ANYBODY EVER CROSSES ME,
I CAN BE *RUTHLESS*!

His booming declaration completed, the Plotmaster
waved his cigar more casually, chuckling softly, as if he
were making a joke with an old friend.

BUT, HEY!
YOU REMEMBER ME, YOU'RE CURIOUS ABOUT
ME.
SO YOU WANT TO ASK A QUESTION OR TWO?

His voice lost its chuckle for an instant as he added:

NOTHING *TOO* PERSONAL, NOW.

The Plotmaster laughed jovially, as if he and Roger were
indeed best buddies. For some reason, Roger thought once
again about what it might mean to have your contract can-
celled.

The Plotmaster paused, waiting. The angelic choir sang
expectantly.

Well, apparently, the big man wanted Roger to ask questions. And, in his time in the Cineverse, Roger had indeed
come up with a few questions.

But being in front of the Plotmaster seemed to call for
more than casual conversation. There must be some question

that Roger should ask first. What was really his biggest concern in all the Cineverse? There was the search for Captain Crusader, concern for his friends—but, really, overriding everything else was the woman who had led Roger into this quest.

That, then, would have to be his first question.

"Um," Roger began, "about Delores—"

But the Plotmaster had already started to speak again, as if he had forgotten he'd ever asked Roger to pose a question.

YOU'RE PROBABLY WONDERING WHY I ASKED
YOU HERE TODAY?

The Plotmaster waved his cigar like a baton, conducting a silent and invisible orchestra, or maybe a very distant chorus.

ROGER, SWEETIE, BABY!
POINT ONE:
YOU REMEMBER ME.

POINT TWO:
YOU'LL LEARN YOUR WAY AROUND THE
CINEVERSE.
DO I NEED TO *SPELL IT OUT* FOR YOU?
IT'S A WINNING COMBINATION.
I'M EXPECTING BIG THINGS OF YOU, ROGER!

What? Roger thought. He was even more confused than back when Delores used to try to explain the Cineverse. Why was he—Roger Gordon of Earth—some kind of winning combination? And, for that matter, he still hadn't asked the Plotmaster about Delores!

The Plotmaster coughed before Roger could think to frame another question.

THERE WAS SOMETHING ELSE, WASN'T THERE?

the Plotmaster asked rhetorically. His hand reached down
to a table that Roger would have sworn hadn't been there
a moment before.

OF COURSE! SILLY OF ME.
I WANTED TO REMIND YOU ABOUT THIS PART
IN THE SCRIPT.
THIS VERY DIFFICULT PART—

He picked up what looked like a thick, bound manuscript.
A script? About Roger? And everybody else, too, probably—including Delores! Roger was astonished. The implications of this were enormous!
The Plotmaster flipped quickly through the pages.

WHERE WAS IT? I HAD IT A MINUTE AGO.
I'M SURE IT WAS IMPORTANT—
SOMETHING ABOUT—LIFE AND DEATH.

He nodded as he finally found his place.

AH—

He looked up as an insistent trilling sounded all around
him.

NOW?
WOULDN'T YOU KNOW IT?
WE'RE JUST GETTING TO KNOW EACH OTHER
AND THE PHONE RINGS.
WELL, ROGER, YOU AND ME, WE'RE BOTH BUSY
MEN, HUH?
I HATE TO RUSH YOU, BUT YOU KNOW—
IMPORTANT CALLS?

Important calls? Roger thought. But the Plotmaster had
been talking about life and death!

WHEN YOU'RE THE PLOTMASTER,
YOU CAN REALLY HAVE YOUR HANDS FULL,
LET ME TELL YOU!

The Plotmaster snapped his fingers again, with the usual echo accompaniment. The angelic choir broke off mid-note. He waved to Roger as he picked up the phone.

LET'S GET TOGETHER AGAIN, SOMETIME SOON!
YOU KNOW I'M COUNTING ON YOU, BOOBALA!

The Plotmaster puffed again, and was surrounded by blue smoke.

But the Plotmaster hadn't told Roger anything! This was not just a dream sequence, Roger realized; it was an anxiety dream sequence!

Roger wasn't going to let this happen. He couldn't let the Plotmaster go before he knew more.

"But—" Roger called.
"But—"
  "But—"
    "But—"
      "But—"
        "But—"
And the echo faded away.

Roger opened his eyes. He was back in the hovel by the lake. He felt hands around his throat as he was once again dragged to his feet. A madwoman stared him in the face.

The dream was over.

"Minsky mensky boobala!" Liv yelled at Roger, every word bursting with hatred.

Roger once again looked at the subtitle.

I HAVE THOUGHT ABOUT THIS FOR A LONG TIME.

"Minsky mensky boobala!" she added. Hadn't she just said that? But the subtitle was different.

WHAT I WOULD DO WHEN YOU CAME BACK TO ME.

Life and death, the Plotmaster had said. Was this the very situation the man with the blue-smoke cigar had wanted to warn him about?

Liv leaned over him. Her breath smelled like she had been eating rotting rodents.

"Mensky minsky granola puffenstuff!"

HOW I COULD MAKE YOU SUFFER THE WAY I DID.

She grabbed him by the back of the neck and pulled him towards her. Roger's first thought was how strong women's hands were in this foreign art film. He thought then for an instant about trying to say something to her again. The word "piglet" came floating into his consciousness. This, when combined with the continuing pain in both his throat and kneecap convinced him that, for now, silence was the best policy.

"Rottentotten nets!"

DEATH IS NOT ENOUGH.

She wasn't going to kill him? Maybe this wasn't the Plotmaster's warning. Roger allowed himself the slightest bit of hope. Maybe his silence was working after all.

"Minsky mensky somethingorother!" she added.

IT HAS TO BE A PARTICULARLY PAINFUL DEATH.

Roger's slight hope evaporated instantaneously. She kicked the door open and dragged him outside before he could further react to the bad news, once again circling both her hands around his neck.

"Oons!" she continued almost cheerfully. "Norts gebort. Minsky providentially voola-voola shebang!"

COME. EVERYTHING IS READY. IT IS PROVIDENTIALLY CO-INCIDENTAL THAT SOMEONE HAS LEFT A BOAT.

Roger caught a quick glimpse of his surroundings as he was tossed outside. There was indeed a small rowboat at the edge of the lake, but it looked in worse repair than the woman's shack, like the faded memory of a craft that once, in the distant past, before six holes had appeared in its hull, could have conceivably floated on the chill gray water.

The pressure left his throat for an instant. Roger felt his

hands being tied tight behind his back, and then the choke-hold was back. In a matter of seconds, he had been dragged down to boatside.

Liv said a single word:

"Krensk."

The subtitle, however, was much longer.

I THINK DEATH BY DROWNING IS ALMOST PUNISHMENT ENOUGH. DEATH BY DROWNING AFTER BEING TRAPPED IN A BURNING BOAT IS EVEN BETTER.

Roger was tossed roughly into the boat, which was filled with dry twigs and leaves. Liv smiled as she pushed the boat out into the lake, then lit a match which in turn ignited an oil-soaked rag.

"Lars!" she called as she tossed the rag into the dried brush. "Tootles!"

Roger struggled, but his hands were firmly tied, the ropes digging cruelly into his flesh. The brush caught fire energetically at the other end of the boat—a fire that would reach him in a matter of seconds, if the ancient, leaky craft didn't sink first.

Oddly enough, the only thing Roger could think of at that moment was that Liv hadn't used the knife.

That's when she threw it at him. He saw the shining blade headed straight for his chest, its cutting edge passing cleanly through the single word of Liv's last subtitle:

GOODBYE.

⥲ 14 ⥲
"Dread Coincidence!"

"Plssm grrsmm!" the gang leader mumbled. "Blssm grssm!"

"You play one more guitar chord," the thin gang member elucidated, "and we'll use our blades on your guitars."

"Yeah!" another of the gang added heavily. "And not just the strings, either!"

Bix Bale and the Belltones stopped strumming abruptly.

Delores stared at the approaching gang, smirks on their faces and weapons of destruction in their hands. Her companions gathered around her, ready to confront this newest threat with everything from royally jungle-trained muscles to canine Wonder Teeth.

But confrontation was not the answer. There had to be some way out of this pattern of battle after battle. If they did nothing but fight, how would they ever find Captain Crusader?

That's when the sand rose up before her. The gang stopped.

"Oh no, you don't," a deep, all-too-familiar voice intoned. "Delores is mine."

The figure was vaguely man-shaped, although slightly taller than most men. Beyond that, Delores could tell nothing, for the figure was entirely coated with sand.

"Scffmmm prfffss drrrtt!" the fellow who mumbled ordered.

His unpleasantly skinny sidekick added in his most sarcastic tone: "The Mumbler wants to know if you guys are scared of a pile of dirt!"

The entire gang jeered at that. Those among the mob intelligent enough to talk added a few comments of their own:

"Yeah—dirt!"

They advanced again.

"Dirt needs to be stomped!"

They brandished knives.

"We'll bulldoze 'im!"

They swung chains.

"We'll ex-ex-uh-excavate 'im!"

They pounded brass knuckles into bloody palms, the pain apparently not reaching their small and distant brains.

"We'll throw him into the ocean and turn him into mud!" the unpleasant skinny fellow added as the gang formed a semicircle half a dozen paces from the sand creature.

But all the monster did was laugh. "I am more than a pile of dirt. Beneath this sandy exterior lurks a heart of pure slime!"

The gang stopped to look at each other.

"Sliffmm?" the Mumbler demanded.

"Nah!" the thin fellow exclaimed. "It can't be that bad."

The gang approached the sand-covered creature, perhaps a bit more tentatively than before.

"I have warned you," the monster replied solemnly. It turned its featureless head toward Delores and her band. "If you would stand a little farther back, it would insure you are out of the line of sludge.'' The creature took a deep breath, then continued hurriedly. ''I dedicate this new work to you, Delores. I call it 'Gang Covered by Slime.' ''

With that, the Slime Monster lifted up what might have been its arms, or possibly its tentacles—it was hard to tell underneath all that crusted sand. The gang rushed forward. One of them whipped a chain across the creature's shoulder. The metal links landed with a dull thud. The monster did not seem to notice.

''I begin!'' the creature announced, and sludge burst forth from the twin points the thing had raised, more like dual hoses than fingers.

Brownish-gray slime covered the gang in a matter of seconds. When they moved, they slipped. When they slipped, they fell. When they spoke, they said only ''glub'' or ''gurgle.''

''My work is done,'' the creature declared proudly.

''Gang Covered by Slime?'' Delores asked.

The monster nodded its sand-covered head (if head it truly was). ''It is my latest creation. I understand that there are those who do not appreciate my art. But I have no choice. It is the artist within me. I must express myself through slime.''

''Hey, that's great!'' one of the tanned, swimsuit-clad lads called. ''You put the Mad Mumbler and his Motorcycle Mob in its place! I think that calls for a song!''

The band started tuning up again. The monster turned to regard the speaker.

''Not unless you want to be covered by slime.''

The guitars ceased strumming even more quickly than they had last time.

''Thank you,'' the monster replied. ''Sometimes my art requires silence.''

''*Glub*,'' the gang members remarked as they rolled around, so that their own, personal slime became sand-coated as well. ''*Gurgle*.''

''You have seen one of my pieces before—the one I titled

'Doctor Dread Covered by Slime,'" the monster continued. "It is so difficult to display my work. Slime is such a transitory form!"

"Not when you add sand!" Zabana observed wryly.

"*Gurgle*," the gang members added from where they still struggled to rise. "*Glub.*"

"That is true," Edward mused. "I had never thought of adding other things to the slime. It gives me whole new sources of inspiration. This could be the first of many. We could call it my 'dirt period.' And it's all because of you, Delores."

Delores didn't know how to answer that. She stared moodily at the gang members. A couple of them had collected enough sand on their persons so that they could finally stand without sliding, their "glubs" and "gurgles" muffled by the extra coating of dirt. She realized, though, that she was only avoiding this Edward thing, hoping against hope that the monster would simply go away. What should she say to this creature to make him understand? For that matter, what did you say to a slime monster under any circumstances?

Edward spoke again before she could come to any decision, a wistful tone to his voice. "It was too bad you had to leave that time we were in the city together, when you were being chased by an incredible number of bad guys, before you could see the work I titled 'An Incredible Number of Bad Guys Simultaneously Coated by Slime.' It may have been my masterpiece—at least of my early, slime-only period."

"Slime as art?" Delores managed at last, knowing that she had to say something. "It is a sobering thought."

"I knew you would see what I was trying to do!" the monster enthused. "Oh, why can't the critics be more like you? Why must the petty art world misunderstand?"

"Is Law of Cineverse!" the jungle prince answered.

The standing gang members had managed, while only falling down once or twice again themselves, to help the rest of their sand-covered fellows to their feet. The entire crew shuffled away from the Slime Monster, in the general direction of the ocean.

"Yip, bark!" Dwight the Wonder Dog interrupted as he leapt about enthusiastically at Louie's side. "Bark, yip, arf!"

The dog's outburst brought Delores back to her senses, beyond slime monsters and sand-covered gang members. They had come to this world for a purpose. Wasn't Captain Crusader supposed to be here someplace?

Louie once again interpreted. "Dwight says that Captain Crusader's been all over this place!"

"He has?" Delores asked, almost too excited to go on. After all this time, and all those worlds, had their quest finally succeeded? "Where is he?" She looked around at a beach full of startled surfers. "Don't anybody move!"

Dwight once again put his nose to the ground. He trotted quickly to an area of packed sand directly in front of the raised bandstand where Bix Bale and the Belltones fearfully watched their instruments.

"Bark! Yip! Arf!" Dwight informed them.

"He's getting close!" Louie exclaimed.

Dwight jumped up onto the bandstand, quickly sniffing at Bix Bale and the Belltones before dismissing them as unworthy of Captain Crusader consideration. Delores frowned. Something was wrong here. Why didn't Captain Crusader, hero among heroes, simply step forward? There was something strange about this whole situation. Did this all have something to do with the Change?

The dog leapt back to the beach, coming within snuffling range of every cluster of surfers and beach bunnies. He galloped over to the Motorcycle Mob, who were washing away sand and slime in the surf, but their smell came up as negative as well. The Wonder Canine even, very briefly, sniffed the Slime Monster, but, after one very astonished "yip!" of disbelief, quickly moved on.

Dwight trotted over to Big Louie. "Yip, yip, yip!" he stated at last. "Arf, arf, arf!"

Now it was Louie's turn to frown. "Dwight says he's somewhere nearby, but he isn't here."

Delores looked at the sidekick, then at the Wonder Dog. Yes, this was definitely odd. It sort of sounded like Captain Crusader was here, and at the same time wasn't here. So where was he? And who was he? This sort of world, full of sand and surf, didn't seem like an obvious hangout for the active hero type—the surroundings here were just too frivolous.

Which, of course, led to other questions. They had come here to find Captain Crusader, but on whose instructions? Dwight the Wonder Dog's? But Delores didn't even know that for sure. What she did know was that Big Louie was giving the orders, supposedly for the Wonder Dog, but since he was the only one who could understand what the dog was saying, who could say who was the mastermind behind this latest phase of their adventures—a sidekick or an animal?

And how well could a mere dog, even one with a Wonder Sense of Smell, track the person who was turning out to be the most elusive hero in the Cineverse? What if Captain Crusader had changed his image once again, as he was so fond of doing? He could be anywhere. He could be hiding in their very midst without them knowing it. Any one of them—well, she knew *she* wasn't Captain Crusader; at least, she was pretty sure of it—but any of the others could be the hero's hero in disguise! Doc, Zabana, even Officer O'Clanrahan, had heroic credentials. Or the Captain could be even more heavily disguised as, say, Big Louie, or one of these kids on the beach!

Delores stopped and stared at the panting canine as she realized he could even be—Dwight the Wonder Dog. It was all too confusing. Why were they here? Who was Captain Crusader? She would have to leave all these questions behind if she were to be of any use at all in their search. In the Cineverse, you sometimes simply had to accept things.

"They're called holes in the plot," Louie assured her, even though she hadn't spoken any of her thoughts aloud.

"Yip yip! Bark arf!" Dwight added.

"Dwight says that this is the right place," Louie interpreted. "We simply have to be patient."

Delores sighed. Now she had both a sidekick and a dog reading her mind. But she realized she might have more immediate problems. The Mad Mumbler and the Motorcycle Mob had cleaned all the sand and slime from their persons and were trudging back up the beach.

"Zabana ready for anything," the jungle prince said as he moved to her side.

"That goesh double for me, misshy!" Doc said as he staggered over to join them.

Oh, no! Delores had feared this very sort of thing. They had been out of action for too long, and something had tipped the balance in the delicate line Doc walked between helpless sobriety and helpless inebriation. She had known it all along, even though she hadn't wanted to admit it: The plot had been too straightforward up to now. Delores was all too aware of the shifts and surprises that lurked out there, especially since the Change. She thought of men wearing hockey masks, and shivered. The longer they searched for Captain Crusader, the more they invited the products of the Change, and Cineverse disaster.

"I'sh the beach," Doc explained as he tried to stand without swaying. "Jush a shmall cashe of shunshtroke."

He fell down, face first, into the sand. He made a gentle *foomph* noise when he hit, immediately followed by snoring.

The unpleasantly skinny gang member laughed. "Look, fellas! They're fainting before we even get to them!"

They all laughed in a way that indicated they had learned nothing from their recent experience with slime.

With the lightning swiftness of a jungle cat, Zabana leapt across the sand, felling the skinny fellow with a single blow.

"Zabana even the odds," the jungle prince announced as he danced back to join the others.

"Vrrbbmm! Zrrrbbbmmm!" the Mumbler screamed.

"What?" one of the gang members asked.

"Huh?" another chimed in.

"That guy in the leopard shorts just decked Sneer!" a third explained. "Sneer was the only one who could understand you!"

"Snrrgggmmmm!" the Mumbler raged. "Fllrrrrggg-mmm!"

The sand rose before them for a second time.

"I would go no farther," the familiar voice warned.

"Snrrzzzzz!" the Mumbler hastily replied. "Frrssrrzzz!"

"So they give me another chance to pursue my art," Edward the slime creature remarked casually. "It is a shame. Their shame, of course. My triumph! I will call it 'The Entire Gang Covered by Slime for a Second Time.' I tell you, whole new vistas are opening for me!" The monster waved one of its appendages in their leader's direction. "And I owe it all to Delores!"

The monster once again trained whatever you might call its upper appendages on the Motorcycle Mob.

"Gglllffrrtttt!" the Mumbler protested.

"Yip! Bark bark bark!" Dwight leapt forward to interrupt the action.

"Wait!" Louie explained. "He says the Mumbler doesn't want to fight!"

"You mean Dwight can interpret what this guy is mumbling about?" Delores demanded.

"Hey, now," Officer O'Clanrahan interjected defensively. "He is Dwight the Wonder Dog, after all."

"Mssrrmm!" the Mumbler insisted.

"Yip, bark yip!" Dwight replied.

"Grrrrssllm?" the Mumbler asked.

"Yip yip, bark, yip!" Dwight answered reassuringly.

"The Mumbler wants to work with us," Louie explained. "It seems it's getting boring on this surfing world—"

That's when there was another explosion, accompanied by blowing sand and blue smoke. Delores considered how, since the Change, nothing ever seemed to stay boring for long (with the exception of one South Sea Paradise).

"Heh heh," someone at the center of the smoke snickered sinisterly. "How"—he hesitated tellingly—"convenient."

Delores felt a tap on her shoulder.

"Is Doctor Dread!" Zabana announced.

Delores looked around.

"Hey, baby," a tall, scrawny surfer said in an artificially deep voice. "What's a nice girl like you doing on a beach like this?"

"Faith and begorrah!" Officer O'Clanrahan chimed in, pointing his nightstick at the archvillain. "The bounder is all alone!"

"Not—" Doctor Dread assured them, "for long."

"What?" Delores whispered incredulously as she stared at this newest intruder in her life.

"What's a nice girl like you doing on—" the surfer started again.

"Why are you asking me that at a time like this?" Delores demanded.

"I had to wait for you to be alone!" the surfer replied defensively. "You're a popular girl."

"Well, you'll have to wait a little longer." Delores turned back to study their nemesis.

"Hey!" the surfer called over her shoulder. "I'm a better catch than somebody completely covered by sand!"

"Are you?" Delores murmured. She was surprised how sincerely she doubted that. But Doctor Dread had begun to hesitate meaningfully again.

"I have been meaning to"—Dread coughed delicately—"see you people again, ever since you"—he coughed twice, and not quite as delicately as before—"attempted to dispose of me on that planet of rabbits."

"Your name's Delores, isn't it?" the surfer insisted.

"Interesting that you should be here," Dread continued,

"the very place my information indicates is the most likely location of Captain Crusader."

"My name's Fast Felix," the surfer went on, despite anything Delores could do to the contrary, "the most romantic surfer on the beach. When I saw you in that evening gown, I knew we were made for each other!"

"You see, the Captain and I have a little"—Dread coughed more softly this time, attempting to put the delicacy back in—"business."

"Well, you've met me," Delores replied to the man behind her.

"Zabana say we take him," the jungle prince announced.

"My thoughtsh exshactly!" Doc added unevenly.

"Now get lost!" Delores finished.

"I wouldn't do that, if I were you. I'm expecting"—this time, Dread tried to hold back the cough—"company."

"But we'll get him before the company arrives!" Officer O'Clanrahan pointed out. "We must prevail. We have Dwight the Wonder Dog!"

"Hard to get, huh?" The scrawny surfer jogged forward so that Delores could see him wriggle his spindly eyebrows. "Fast Felix especially likes women in evening dresses who play hard to get."

"Oh, very well, if you"—Dread paused to clear his throat—"insist. Say, you there in black leather."

"Pptttzzzzmmmm!" the Mumbler declared. His gang paid no attention.

"Us?" one of the members of the Motorcycle Mob asked.

"Of course," Dread continued smoothly. "How would you like to be"—the cough was back—"among the future rulers of the Cineverse?"

"Wrrssfff!" the Mumbler yelled. His gang looked the other way.

"So, babe," Fast Felix insisted. "What do you say?"

"Us?" another mobster replied.

"I knew you'd catch on," Dread purred. "Bright fellows. Very well." He paused for another hack, then pointed casually to Delores and her fellows. "Deal with them!"

Fast Felix ran a hand lightly down Delores' spangled sleeve. "I'll show you sand and surf you've never seen before—"

The gang once again approached. Delores pushed Fast Felix out of her way and joined the line of her allies, all once again ready to do battle with the forces of evil. They had to be doubly wary now. She expected more blue smoke explosions at any second. But would those explosions contain more minions of Doctor Dread, or would they bring Captain Crusader? Whatever happened, she knew for certain, they were facing their moment of decision.

"Hey, babe," Delores heard behind her. "Fast Felix doesn't take no—"

"This is the end of the line for you, Doctor Dread!" Officer O'Clanrahan announced.

"Oh my, no. This is only"—Dread paused to smile evilly—"the beginning."

≈ 15 ≈
"Wave of Terror!"

He barely managed to duck the knife. The smoke and fire seemed to have spoiled the woman's aim, unless it was the fact that the boat had sunk an inch or two since she'd thrown her weapon.

Once again, all of Roger's life threatened to flash before his eyes. He remembered Gloria, and Fiona, and Charlene, and Daisy. But he couldn't sink into reminiscence. There still might be some way out of his predicament. He had to do it, for Delores, Captain Crusader, the Earth, the Cineverse, maybe even the Plotmaster, if Roger could ever figure out what the guy had been talking about—and he had to do it for himself. He didn't want to die in the world of a Foreign Art Film, especially after that dream sequence. For all he knew, once he drowned, or was burned, or was stabbed to death, his ghost would be trapped here in the symbolic sky, skipping after the all-nun band. His mind wandered back to Lulu, and Karen, and Clarissa.

No! He had to think this through. He'd escaped from other tight spots before—well, perhaps they hadn't been as tight as this one. He simply had to look at his predicament in as objective a manner as possible. There must be some way out. Mere hours ago, Dr. Dee Dee Davenport had declared him to be "incredibly lucky." Roger would hate to prove her wrong.

He pushed thoughts of Tanya and Rachel and Sophia from his head and listed his problems. Liv had missed with her knife, so that meant all he had to contend with was a sinking boat that was rapidly being consumed by fire. That, and the fact that the new Captain Crusader Ring he'd gotten from the computer was a dud, so he couldn't get out that way, besides which, his hands were tied, so that there was no way he could get to the ring. His mind drifted to Daphne, and Sheri, and Theodora.

But no—the Plotmaster seemed to think Roger had something special going for him. Roger tried to quickly remember the points the big guy with the blue-smoke cigar had made. One was that Roger actually remembered the Plotmaster. The other was something about how, with time, Roger would learn his way around the Cineverse.

No he wouldn't. Roger was going to burn up in a boat. The fire felt awfully hot on his face. At least the flames didn't affect his feet, probably because both his sneakers were already under six inches of water.

Wait a minute! All this stuff about the Plotmaster had almost made him forget—a minute ago, he'd been thinking about his new Captain Crusader Ring! But he also had an *old* Captain Crusader Decoder Ring. Sure, it was defective, but it worked after a fashion, and even the Beach Party surfing world was preferable to existential death!

The ring was only a few inches away, in the breast pocket of his jogging suit. He leaned forward. Was there any possible way he could reach it? His jogging jacket bunched up towards him. For the first time ever, he was grateful for that spare tire that had started around his waist in the last couple of years, that same layer of fat that now pushed his jacket up his chest.

He looked down, and saw that he had left the pocket unzipped. He calmed a momentary panic. He could have lost the ring, but he hadn't. It was still there. He could feel the hard lump of ring and gum, with the point of his chin.

He looked up to see the flames racing down both sides of the boat, burning everything to the waterline, where water and fire turned to steam. Steam and smoke were everywhere. Maybe he wouldn't be drowned or burned after all. Maybe he'd be boiled, instead.

He had to get the ring now. He bent down farther than he had since he was seventeen.

His heart leapt as his tongue tasted hard, stale gum. He had reached the ring! With a superhuman effort, he managed to inch his chin even farther down, grasping the cheap plastic ring in his teeth.

The bow of the boat disappeared beneath the surface of the lake. This was his last chance.

"See oo eh ee unny aa-ers!" he managed.

To his relief, the smoke turned blue.

The smoke drifted away on an ocean breeze.

The ring dropped from his teeth as his mouth opened in shock.

Was *everybody* here?

"Roger!" Delores yelled.

"Delores!" he yelled back.

"Dr. Dread!" Big Louie pointed.

"Louie?" Roger asked.

"Mffffmm!" the Mad Mumbler demanded.

"Congratulashuns!" Doc slurred, his voice somewhat muffled by the sand.

"Roger!" Delores called.

"Delores!" he called back.

"We got a job," a member of the Motorcycle Mob muttered.

"Mfffmm!" the Mumbler interrupted.

"Zabana," the jungle prince declared as he moved to block their path.

"Oh, yeah?" the mob member retorted.

"Slime," came the answer of the sand-covered one who now stood next to Zabana.

"Oh, yeah," the mob member agreed.

"Roger!" Delores laughed.

"Delores!" He laughed back.

"But Dr. Dread!" Louie insisted.

"Mfffffmmmmmmm!" the Mumbler interrupted.

"Yip! Arf!" Dwight elucidated.

"Say," Roger asked, "isn't that Dwight the Wonder Dog?"

"Everybody knows Dwight—" Officer O'Clanrahan began.

"Oh, Roger," Delores whispered sweetly.

"Oh, Delores," was Roger's husky reply.

"But really!" Louie jumped up and down. "Doctor Dread!"

"Where?" Roger asked.

"Hey, Roger-Dodger!" Brian called as he trotted up.

"Are we glad to see you!" Frankie added as he tagged along.

"Under!" Louie pointed down.

"Under?" Roger asked. He looked down at the remains of his boat.

"The Cowabunga-munga!" Brian called.

"Any minute now!" Frankie added.

"The Cowabunga-munga?" Delores asked.

"Oh, Delores." Roger shrugged.

"Oh, Roger," Delores replied.

"DOCTOR DREAD!" Louie screamed.

"Oh, that's right." Roger shook his head. "Under?"

"The boat!" Louie explained. "When you appeared!"

"Under the boat?" Roger asked in disbelief.

"Hit right on snakeskin target," Zabana added admiringly.

"Couldna done better myshelf!" Doc admitted.

"Yip! Arf! Yip!" Dwight cheered.

"Is he dead?" Roger asked, frowning at the bits of charred wood beneath him. As usual when he traveled with the Captain Crusader Decoder Ring, he had brought his most immediate recent surroundings along with him. But he couldn't see Doctor Dread at all.

"Unfortunately, no." Delores shook her head. "You can't kill a supervillain that easily."

"Mffffffffffffffmmmmmmmmmmmmmmmmmmmmm!" the Mumbler interrupted once again.

"Yip, yip, bark!" Dwight insisted.

"Oh!" Louie remarked. "Is that what he wants to do?"

KABOOM! the air exploded.

"What was that?" Brian worried.

"More blue smoke?" Frankie joined in.

"Ah hahahaha! Ah hahahaha!" a new voice laughed.

"Menge the Merciless?" Delores asked.

The smoke cleared.

It was more than Menge.

"What are you doing here, worm?" yet another voice added.

"Cripes!" Big Louie yelled. "It's my sister!"

"My, it's—Roger, isn't it?" Bertha asked coyly.

"Roger?" Delores questioned.

"Delores!" Roger insisted.

"I'm so glad you're still here," Bertha cooed.

"Gee, Bertha," Louie interrupted. "Have you turned a new leaf?"

"Quiet, worm! No, I was afraid Roger would have met his death before I had a chance to *use* him!" She regarded her prey with half-closed eyes as she made grasping motions with her hands.

"Don't forget about me," another voice stated flatly.

"Professhor Peril!" Doc managed.

"With Mort the Killer Robot!" Officer O'Clanrahan observed.

"Yip! Arf! Bark!" Dwight added.

"And Diablo," Louie explained, "the Gorilla with the Mind of a Man!"

"Thank you for the introduction," Peril replied brusquely. "This is, of course, your doom."

"Give or take fifteen minutes spent behind a nearby sand dune," Bertha added lasciviously.

"Ah hahahaha!" Menge the Merciless added for good measure. "Ah hahahaha!"

"Roger!" Delores called, a new determination in her voice.

"Delores!" he agreed, putting an arm around her shoulder and hugging her tight.

"I don't think any of this—" Frankie began.

"—is going to happen," Brian added. "Especially with the Cowabunga-munga—"

"—a few minutes away?" Frankie completed the thought. "I do know what is—"

"—going to happen, though," Brian picked up on it. "Yeah!"

They both shouted the next sentence together:

"It's time for a song!"

This time, things were so confused that Bix Bale and the Belltones were well into their three-chord progression before there were any threats to their continued existence. By then, of course, it was far too late. With guitar, bass, and drum once again singing across the sand, the spell of the surfing world had taken hold.

This time, Frankie started the song:

"Roger's back and he's our fave
  'Cause it's almost time for the great big wave!
  He'll be the king of all our turf
  When he shows he can really surf!"

This was followed by the usual "heys," "nanny-nannies," and drumbeats. Roger tried not to listen. It was difficult, though, with all those people dancing around him. Delores certainly looked stunning in that spangled evening dress, but then, he was sure she'd look good in anything. Some of the others looked a little stranger as they fell under the music's spell. Doctor Dread was moving around with a sort of snakeskin shimmy, while Bertha, still eyeing Roger, was performing something that appeared to be a particularly violent form of the polka. Officer O'Clanrahan was doing the waltz, while Dwight, on his hind legs, was waltzing along. Everyone was swirling around him to that relentless surfing beat. But Roger couldn't let himself be seduced by the jangly rock and roll. He had to talk to Delores, tell her about the Plotmaster, save the Cineverse, and that was just for starters! But he knew, if he let his concentration waver for an instant, he too would be caught up in the music, on his way to face the largest wave that ever was!

Brian took the next verse:

> "Roger hasn't got a thing to fear;
>   He'll be the surfer of the year!
>   So everybody now stand and cheer;
>   The Cowabunga-munga is almost here!"

"Hey!" everybody yelled. Roger frowned. Something was different about the dancers. For a moment, he thought they weren't moving as much as before. But then he realized the real difference—he was dancing along with them! No! He tried to stop, to force himself free of the music's spell. But how could you just sit there when they were playing surf guitar?

Frankie got the next verse:

> "Some guys leave this big wave alone,
>   They say it's a good way to break a bone;

A wave so fierce that away they're blown,
But Roger will handle it on his own.''

Hey! Yeah, he was really dancing now, and with Delores, the cutest bunny on the beach! Roger didn't know when he'd felt this happy. He wanted to do something big, something important!

Brian's singing gave him an idea.

"Some guys on the wave they will not glide.
They claim one that size is suicide!
They say they'd rather face cyanide,
But Roger's going to take this wave in stride.''

"Hey!" Roger shouted along with everybody else. What a good idea!

Why was he standing around on this beach, worrying about stupid things like the Cineverse?

It was time to go out and catch that wave!

$\approx$ 16 $\approx$
"Flaming Death Goes to the Seashore!"

Now where had Roger put his surfboard? For the life of him, he couldn't remember.

"Hey, Roger-Dodger, the time has come!" Brian shouted.

"Yeah, man!" Frankie agreed. "It's time to face the Cowabunga-munga!"

"Yeah!" Roger laughed, almost drunk with the challenge. "It's time to ride me a wave!"

"Hey, guys!" A rather pale and underfed surfer in snakeskin swimming trunks trotted toward them through the sand. "I've got Roger's device—er, I mean—we've got Roger's board, man!"

"My board!" Roger exclaimed. So that's what happened to it! "Well, hey guys! Bring it here!"

"Okay, kids!" the snakeskin-suited surfer called. "Let's make the scene with the board!"

Nothing happened. All the surfers and beach bunnies stood around and looked at each other.

"Professor! Menge!" the sickly surfer yelled. "I mean—er—where are you guys?"

"We're back here!" a curt voice called from the rear of the crowd. "Do you want the device?"

"Yeah, sure!" This new surfer seemed to be sweating an awful lot for someone standing so close to the sea breezes. "That's what I said. Bring the board!"

"The what?" the other voice asked.

"The board!" the new surfer repeated. "The surfboard! Roger's surfboard!"

There was no reply.

"The device!" the surfer yelled.

"Oh, yeah, sure!" the other voice finally called back. "The surfboard! Got it right here. Roger's surfboard!"

Two men in baggy swimsuits ran through the crowd, carrying something that was long, flat, and red. Neither one of them looked like they saw much of the sun, either. The fellow in front was compactly built and moved with quick, nervous energy; the fellow behind him, who was bald and a bit on the flabby side, had to struggle to keep up.

"Here it is, Doctor Dread!" the compact fellow announced as they approached. "The dev—I mean, the surfboard!"

"Doctor Dread?" Roger repeated with a frown. There was something about that name, something that didn't belong on a world of sand and surf.

"Don't listen to those guys," the snakeskinned surfer replied with a nervous smile. "You can call me Dreaddy."

"Dreaddy," Roger repeated with a smile. Yes, that name sounded much better.

"And these are my friends," Dreaddy went on, "the Prof and Mengy. They're the guys who"—he hesitated for some reason—"worked on your board."

"Mengy?" the flabby fellow complained.

"Ixnay!" Dreaddy said out of the corner of his mouth. "Ou'reyay an urfersay!"

"Oh, yeah!" The flabby fellow laughed and waved halfheartedly. "Mengy!"

"Roger?" a lyrically feminine voice whispered in his ear. "Could I talk with you?"

"Okay, babe," Roger said as he turned to the young woman. "I don't have much time. I've got a wave to catch."

She smiled at him as he turned—the kind of smile that would melt the heart of even the most hardened surfer. Her spangled evening dress sparkled in the midday sun. Didn't he know this girl from somewhere? A name floated past the sound of waves and the memory of surf guitar—Delores. That was it. Roger was glad to see her again. Even though she wasn't wearing a bikini, Delores wouldn't look out of place anywhere.

"I understand," she reassured him. She pushed her long blond hair out of her eyes, hair that shone in the wind and sun. "But I must talk to you."

"But, girly!" Dreaddy insisted. "Roger's got to get ready for his surfing challenge!"

"Yeah, Roger," Mengy added. "You haven't even taken a look at your new board."

"Yes," the Prof continued as he and Mengy lifted the surfboard between them. "We've added some very interesting modifications."

They had, too. It was the strangest board Roger had ever seen, especially with the red tubes along the side, and the lump of plastic over the rear fin.

"Hey, babe!" another voice interrupted. "Why'd you split the scene?"

"Oh, no," Delores whispered. In a much louder voice, she shouted at the newcomer: "Would you kindly get out of my life?"

"Oho!" the tall, tanned, and slightly awkward newcomer replied. "Spirited—that's the way Fast Felix likes 'em!"

"Roger," Delores continued, "could we go somewhere else to talk?"

"Well, gee, babe, if I didn't have this surfing duel—"

"But that's right, Roger-Dodger!" Dreaddy insisted. "You do have this surfing duel, and this special board, which you'd better try out right now!"

"Hey, cutie!" Fast Felix interrupted. "Who is this new guy? How can you turn your back on the greatest lover on the beach?"

"Who's the greatest lover on the beach?" another woman's voice loudly demanded. "Outta my way!"

Surfers screamed and scattered as another newcomer trod heavily through the sand.

The oily smile fell from Felix's face as he turned to look at the woman, who now stood all alone.

"My name is Bertha," she growled gutturally, "and if I want you, you're mine."

Felix started to shake. He opened his mouth, but no sound issued forth. Roger had to admit that Bertha cut an imposing figure. Maybe it was that six feet six inches of height. Maybe it was the pink bikini on that thick, muscle-laden body. It made her look as sexy as a Sherman tank. Perhaps, Roger considered, pink was not her color.

"Who's that?" Roger asked.

"Oh," Dreaddy said lightly, "just another one of my beach buddies." He cleared his throat delicately. "Bertha, dearest? Perhaps now is not the best time—"

She shook her head and pointed at Felix. "So you're the best lover? Prove it!"

"Prove it?" Utter fear allowed Felix to find his voice again. "Oh, wow. Well, you know—I talk a lot. Maybe I'm not the best—"

"No one backs down from Big Bertha!" she announced as she grabbed Felix with both of her ham-sized hands and lifted him from his feet. "Let's see what you're made of."

He squirmed, but only for an instant. There was a loud

crunch, like the smashing of cartilage and bone. Fast Felix went limp.

"Typical shoddy merchandise." Beach Bunny Bertha tossed the remains over her shoulder.

"Anybody else?" she asked.

All the other surfers started walking casually toward some other beach.

"But about this surfboard," Dreaddy continued as if nothing had happened.

"It's really customized!" Mengy joined in as he pointed to the flame decals.

"It was providentially coincidental," the Prof explained, "that we could get parts from this old car and rocket ship that were sitting around on the beach."

"Yeah!" Mengy agreed. "It's amazing what you can scavenge from a rocket ship."

"But, Roger—" Delores began.

"Hey, you've got to get going!" Brian exclaimed.

"Yeah!" Frankie added. "The Cowabunga-munga waits for no man!"

"So take the board," Dreaddy insisted.

Mengy and the Prof held the six-foot-long surfboard out to him. Why did Roger feel such trepidation as he touched the polished red wood?

"Good," Dreaddy purred as Roger accepted the board. "I promise you you'll have no"—there came that hesitation again—"regrets."

"With this board, you can't lose," the Prof explained.

"Let's just say you'll go over in a big way," Mengy cheerfully added. "Ah hahahaha!"

"Yes, I think you'll find the results quite—" Dreaddy paused yet again. Roger wondered if maybe the surfer had a problem speaking in public.

"—explosive," he finished at last.

The three pasty surfers smiled at each other as if they shared a private joke.

Delores shook his shoulder. "Roger! Can't you see—"

"Listen!" Brian and Frankie shouted together.

Everyone stopped talking. Some of the surfers who had fled at Big Bertha's recent assault started to drift back. The birds had stopped singing, the ocean breezes had ceased abruptly—even the waves seemed somehow muted—but it wasn't silent. There was a sound so low that Roger almost felt it more than heard it, a deep rumble that seemed to fill the whole line of the western horizon, rising from an ocean that still appeared deceptively calm.

Brian and Frankie whispered together:

"The Cowabunga-munga!"

"Lrsssgrrssmm!" called a muscular fellow in black leather swimming trunks. He carried a jet-black surfboard.

A dog barked nearby.

"The Mumbler says its time for your duel!" a small man in a double-breasted suit explained.

"But, Roger—" Delores tugged on his arm with a desperate insistence.

"Get away from him, you hussy!" another, very deep woman's voice demanded.

Roger turned around and almost dropped the board. Big Bertha was bearing down on him.

"Roger's going out to face the biggest wave that ever was," Bertha asserted. "A wave he may never come back from. I think he's going to need a good luck kiss. And I'm just the kisser to give it!"

Delores turned a very funny shade of red. She leaned over and gave Roger a quick kiss on the nose. "I may not be able to convince you of your folly," she whispered, "but I can save you from this."

She turned to Bertha and shouted: "I warn you—I've been to Hero School!"

Balancing his board with his right hand, Roger touched his nose with his left.

Shouts of "girl fight!" came from the growing crowd of surfers.

His nose tingled where her lips had brushed it.

Delores took three graceful steps across the sand.

He would remember that tingle anywhere.

Bertha stomped forward, murder in her eyes, muscles rippling between the two strips of pink.

That woman was not simply *any* Delores. She was *his* Delores! As he was her Roger! It was like something out of *Sleeping Beauty*—her kiss had brought him back to his senses!

"This is getting serious!" Brian yelled.

"Bertha, this is," Dreaddy chimed in, hardly hesitating at all, "—counterproductive."

Wait a moment. That wasn't Dreaddy. It was Doctor Dread, looking particularly anemic in his snakeskin swimwear. And, among the crowd of surfers, Roger could see Zabana—who actually fit in quite well—and Officer O'Clanrahan, and Louie, and Dwight the Wonder Dog, all of whom were rather easier to spot. That meant they were all back together again. It also meant that there was no way he was going to go out and get himself killed facing some humongous wave. He had no idea how to surf! Roger let go of the board. It fell to the sand with a dull thud.

"But Roger!" Frankie pleaded. "The Cowabunga-munga won't wait!"

"I want what I want," Bertha announced, "and no one will stand in my way."

"Fllmshrrssmm!" the Mad Mumbler demanded.

"Erthabay!" Dread demanded. "Ou'reyay inay ouble-tray!"

"I don't care," she snarled back, pounding her grape-fruit-sized fist into her other large and muscular hand. "My love"—pound—"will not"—pound—"be denied."

Dwight the Wonder Dog barked something.

"At lasht!" Doc called from somewhere around the surfers' feet. "A showdown!"

"There's only one way to handle this," Frankie announced.

"That's your cue, Bix!" Brian added.

And the surfing song began all over again. Frankie sang it:

> "Roger's gonna grab that big wave,
>   He might be heading for a water grave!
>   That's why our Roger's just a surfing fool;
>   That's why we think he's pretty cool!"

"Hey!" everybody yelled as usual. But the song wasn't going to work this time. Roger was all too aware of the ever-increasing rumble that came from the sea. He had places to go, people to see, meetings with the Plotmaster to describe.

But Brian was already into the next verse:

> "If he's not careful, in that wave he'll crash,
>   And tons of water will upon him smash.
>   What happens next is not pristine;
>   And that's why Roger is pretty keen."

"Hey!" everybody joined in. Roger smiled a bit at the insistent beat. Actually, when he thought of it again, that ever-growing rumble didn't interfere with the song at all. It worked more like accompaniment, like a bass guitar and a tom-tom drum on a really good stereo system.

> "Everybody let's jump and shout,
>   And hope that Roger does not wipe out,
>   For that to him would be sure doomsday,
>   And that's why Roger is so okay."

Roger sighed. They had been playing this song for so long, he sort of thought of it as an old friend. It would be a shame for a surfboard, especially a board as state-of-the-art as his, to go unused.

"Roger!" Delores yelled as he squatted down to lift his surfboard from the sand.

Dreaddy, Mengy, and the Prof smiled at him as they danced. Delores waved frantically from where she danced behind them.

Roger took a step toward the ocean, then stopped. His left hand wanted to jerk away from the surfboard, as if the red painted wood were lethal to the touch. His right hand punched the sun-drenched air before him, impatient to get out there and face that wave if it was the last thing he did. Why was this so perplexing? Surfers weren't supposed to think!

But Delores was still trying to tell him something.

That's when Frankie launched into another verse about if he hit his head Roger would be dead but he doesn't care if he flops so that's why he was the tops. By the time the crowd had gotten around to shouting "Hey!" he had made his decision.

He wouldn't have a chance for the Cowabunga-munga again.

"Frzzm!" his challenger insisted as the leather-suited muscleman ran out into the waves.

A giant wave, hundreds of feet high. One man against the force of countless tons of water, with enough destructive force to annihilate this beach and everyone on it. How could he refuse an adventure like that? Roger would never forgive himself if he backed down from the ultimate surfing challenge.

Maybe, though, he might want to say a final word to Delores.

He looked around for the beautiful young woman, but, right where he thought she should be, there stood a new pair of surfers, even stranger looking than Dreaddy and his crew. One of them was entirely covered in shining silver, as if his skin were made of metal, while the other's face and body were completely covered by coarse brown hair.

"Who are those guys?" Roger asked uncertainly.

"Nothing to worry about," the Prof assured him. "That's just Mort the Killer—uh—Surfer, and Diablo, the—er—Surfer with the Mind of a Man. They're here to make sure no one interferes with your facing the Cowabunga-munga."

Oh. He had heard those names somewhere before. Or maybe something like those names. There was something about those names—why was everything making him uneasy?

Brian started another verse:

"Now Roger he is on his own,
    If he wipes out, he's blood and bone—"

That was it. Roger didn't need any more coaxing. As soon as the song resumed, all his doubts were gone. He pulled off his socks and sneakers, balanced the board atop his head and ran down the beach.

Brian kept on singing:

"Yeah, he may just be smashed to bits
    But with us he'll always be a hit."

Roger fully agreed. It was time to catch a wave. He jumped atop his board and quickly paddled out into the sea. It was difficult to concentrate, though, and the paddling seemed to get harder as the music grew fainter. Soon, it was difficult to do anything much except listen to that ever-increasing roar in his ears. From the sound, it was going to be the biggest wave Roger had ever seen.

He redoubled his efforts, paddling as fast as he could. The roar was so loud now that it drowned out any traces of the surf guitar behind him. It was harder still to paddle when there was no music at all.

His challenger paddled by Roger, the other's motor-cycle-trained muscles pushing the water out of his way. But Roger had to win this surfing duel! The honor of the beach was at stake! And he wasn't going to do it staring at the other guy's back. If there was no music to urge him on, he would have to urge himself. He would have to make his own music. Roger tried singing a verse off the top of his head:

> "Here it comes, the Cowabunga;
>   Gotta get there, ain't gettin' younga.
>   Gotta paddle, can't be a fool.
>   Gotta finish this surfin' duel!"

It may have been a little rough around the edges, but he thought the verse was pretty good for a first effort.

"Hey!" he shouted, wishing he could somehow hear the surfers back on shore shouting along with him. He knew the music had helped his paddling—he had pulled alongside his opponent by the end of the second couplet. He glanced over his shoulder, and was startled to see how far he had come from the shore in one short verse—the people back there looked like nothing more than tiny specks on an endless strip of sand.

He realized he must have discovered a Law of the Beach—things happened when you sang. It was only logical, considering all the rules he'd confronted elsewhere in the Cineverse. He thought of singing another verse to really get ahead in this surfing duel, but stopped as he listened to the wave—the roar was so loud now, he'd have to shout to be heard.

That's when he looked up and saw the Cowabunga-munga, and all thoughts of surfing duels left his head.

It was not a wave—it was much too large for that. It was more like someone had taken a five-hundred-foot-long knife and cut the ocean in half, and then stuck one piece on top of the other—and the top piece was coming straight for Roger! It was a wall of water, looking as solid as a mile of glass, its very top hidden in a mist that nudged the undersides of the clouds.

The Cowabunga-munga; it certainly lived up to its name. Roger guessed the legendary wave was still over a mile away, but it stretched the length of the horizon, as if it had already conquered the ocean and everything within it, and was coming to take him next.

Roger blinked. What was he doing here? He didn't know how to surf. Even if he did, there was a wall of water out there so huge that it was probably unsurfable. Delores had tried to warn him away. Why hadn't he listened to her? But he knew why—it was that infernal surfing music! That beach party beat had kept him under its spell until he had woken up to the reality of the Cowabunga-munga!

Roger glanced down at the surfboard that he sat upon, and his disquiet turned to despair. It was even worse than he feared. He remembered how Doctor Dread had described this board as "customized," but Roger had been too far gone under the surfing spell to realize the true meaning of Dread's additions!

Even half-gone into surf mania, Roger had noticed the board's special auxiliary pipes, and that odd lump of plastic over the rear fin. Now, though, looking at this customizing in the clear light of total panic, he realized that the "pipes" weren't pipes at all; they were sticks of dynamite wrapped in waterproof tape. And that lump around the fin looked an awful lot like plastic explosive. And why hadn't Roger noticed the wires before? One red, one black, they led from the plastic lump to a small digital clock taped between the board and the dynamite, a clock that read eleven fifty-seven—three minutes to twelve!

Roger had seen enough movies to know what happened at twelve. Doctor Dread and his cronies had prepared for every contingency. The thing he sat on top of wasn't a surfboard; it was a bomb. He had three minutes to live.

Roger realized that this must have been what the Plot-master was warning him about.

He looked up again. The Cowabunga-munga was not

only huge, it was fast, and it was coming straight toward him.

Roger swallowed, the salty taste of sea spray on his tongue. Maybe he didn't have three minutes to live after all.

☛ 17 ☚
"Captain Crusader's Secret!"

Thoughts of Alina and Theresa filled Roger's head. Not to mention Phyllis and Sandra and Rebecca and—

Roger stopped himself. He was acting like he was going to die. Well, he had been through a lot in the Cineverse—perhaps nothing quite as imposing as the Cowabunga-munga—but, still, he wasn't dead. Yet. And, now that he thought of it, he really didn't know if this was the incredibly horrible situation that the Plotmaster had meant to warn him about. The way things were going for Roger in the Cineverse lately, he had about four of these incredibly horrible situations in the average afternoon.

The wave-to-end-all-waves roared towards him.

Well, maybe this situation was marginally worse.

Still, he had gotten out of tough spots before by using his ring. And he had two rings now! True, one of them didn't work at all, unless it really did force people to tell the truth, especially whether or not they were Captain Crusader, as Dr. Dee Dee Davenport claimed. However, Roger didn't believe he could exact any worthwhile confessions from a rapidly approaching wall of water.

The other ring, now, did work, in a very limited way. It would send him to the surfing world. Where he already was. Which was also utterly useless. Unless, Roger remembered, you dropped the ring in exactly the right way—as Dee Dee had a couple of times to lead them to her world and the Institute of Very Advanced Science. And Roger had managed to drop one of these rings once, and had landed back on Earth!

So he could escape. The ring would send him home, if he could handle it just so. True, he had no particular desire to go back to Earth, but it was certainly better than death, wasn't it? Besides which, he would swear there was another Captain Crusader Decoder Ring somewhere in his mother's house, so it was possible—even if he managed to lose the gum-repaired ring in his escape—that he could still make it back to the Cineverse.

Now, the question was, could he remember how Dee Dee had saved them before? And could he do it again? It had something to do with turning the dial and dropping the ring. As Roger recalled, saying "Oops!" might be a required part of the procedure as well.

He looked up at the ever-approaching wave. It was certainly worth a try. At this point, anything was worth a try.

He pulled the ring-and-chewing gum combination from his pocket. He twisted the dial, then tossed the ring into the air.

"Oops!" he shouted hopefully as he tried to catch it. The ring slipped between his fingers, bounced off the board, and fell into the sea.

There was no blue smoke. There was only the Cowabunga-munga, roaring his way, ton upon ton of relentless, churning destruction. And he had just lost his only chance of escape.

Roger thought of Valerie and Vickie and Vanessa—

No! He still wasn't ready to accept death. There had to be some way out of here. The Plotmaster had suggested that knowledge was the key. At least that's what Roger thought the Plotmaster had suggested. He simply had to think like a movie—more specifically, a surfing movie! If there was one thing he should have learned during his sojourn in the Cineverse, it was that things were not fixed in the same way they were on Earth. Here, the plots were mutable to a certain extent, depending on anything from the appearance of a new character on the scene to the decision of somebody to sing a song.

Sing a song? That sort of thing really seemed to work around here. It had certainly gotten Roger out on a surf-board. And, still under that surfing spell, when he had sung a verse all on his own, he had found himself even further at sea. He had already used this rule of the surfing world. And he could use it again.

Roger grinned up at the rapidly approaching Cowabunga-munga. The solution was obvious once he thought of it. If you didn't like what was happening to you, sing about it!

Water stretched before him as far as he could see. The Cowabunga-munga was almost on top of him. If he was going to do something about it, he'd better sing it now.

Roger had to sing so loud, it was more like screaming:

> "The wave it thinks it's got me beat.
> But this here surfer takes the heat!
> He's gonna make this wave his own;
> The Cowabunga, he'll ride home."

Roger looked up at the wall of water. It was everywhere. The wave-to-end-all-waves rushed relentlessly forward, like Niagara Falls on wheels, leaving Roger small and pitiful before a curtain of water that was about to cover the world.

But wait! High up on that never-ending wave, did Roger see a patch of blue sky? Yes, the wave seemed to be breaking in half, the ramparts opening to allow Roger a chance to enter—to surf on in. And he was sure it was the song that had done it.

Now, though, how did he catch the wave and ride it? It only took him a second to decide—there was really no choice, after all—he would have to let the song do that as well. He stood on his board and screamed out another verse as the wave thundered to either side of him.

> "Come on Roger, let's hear a shout,
> 'Cause he's one surfer that won't wipe out!
> Yeah, he's a fellow who'll be your fave,
> 'Cause here he goes to catch that wave!"

It wasn't great poetry, but it worked. He could feel the water swell underneath the board, lifting him up higher and higher on the face of the great wave.

He saw a flash of flesh color from the corner of his eye. Roger risked a glance behind. It was the fellow they called the Mad Mumbler, balanced on his board, riding in Roger's wake—and he wasn't singing at all. Roger was impressed. That fellow could really surf!

Together, they reached the heights of the Cowabunga-munga. Roger broke through the spray and out of the great wave's shadow, into the sunlight high above the world. Seagulls circled nearby, cheering him on with their cries. He was surfing with all the aplomb of Frankie Avalon! He couldn't believe it.

That's when one of his feet slipped. He fell to one knee.

Roger managed to crush the small seed that wanted to blossom into panic inside his chest. Panic was the very thing he could not do. He had had a moment of doubt, and it had almost broken the concentration he had built through song. He had to believe in what he was doing. It was crucial to his survival in the Cineverse!

Besides, he had other problems. He may have conquered the wave for the moment, but there was still the bomb. His other foot slipped ever so slightly as he thought about the

red board beneath him, the one equipped with enough ex-
plosives to blow him up ten times over if he had too great
an impact in the pounding surf, or—if he managed to stay
alive that long—until the timer ran out! The villains had
obviously considered everything—everything, that is, save
Roger's penchant for song!

He glanced down at the timer, and saw there was only a
minute left. This was it, then, his moment of musical truth.
But he had to make sure no last-minute doubts crept in about
his surfing. It wouldn't do him any good to defuse the bomb
if he wiped out in the process. If he was to survive, that
new verse would have to be a masterpiece of concentration
and balance. He had to defuse the bomb while reasserting
his surfing prowess.

Slowly, but careful to maintain that all-important surfing
beat, Roger began again:

> "Now, some folks think Roger's a fool,
> Want him to lose this surfing duel!
> But the bomb's a dud, it just can't last;
> It's Roger who's a surfing blast!"

He risked a glance down at his surfboard. The clock
stopped. The wires sprang free and spiraled off into the
foam. The watertight tape loosened, and the dynamite was
instantly sodden with saltwater. The plastic explosive
slipped beneath the sea. The song had worked, and Roger's
conveyance had gone from bomb to board.

He tossed in another verse for good measure;

> "Hey this guy is really neat;
> He rides the waves with both his feet.
> No one beats him on his turf!
> So come on Roger, surf surf surf!"

Yeah! Roger laughed. He was really moving now. Wind
in his hair, spray in his face. One man against the elements,

surfing his way to glory. That was the way it was supposed
to be! He heard faint cheers from the beach ahead. The
Cowabunga-munga had brought him considerably closer to
his hero-worshipping throng. The surfers on shore had been
transformed from flyspecks to fairly good-sized ants. Roger
even thought he could recognize some of them as they
rightfully cheered him in his great deed. That tall blond
woman in the shining evening dress—that was Delores!

Delores?

Wait a minute. He was no surfer fighting against the
elements. The only great deed he was involved in was stay-
ing alive. He was buying into this whole surfing world
again—this time a victim of his own surfing songs! Roger
had to be careful. The use of power in the Cineverse seemed
to be a tricky thing. One way or another, the more you
invested in a world, the more you became a part of that
place's reality.

A wave washed across his feet. Roger almost fell off the
surfboard. Now he wasn't being positive enough! The de-
mon doubt had almost done him in again.

"Turf, surf, wave, fave!" Roger chanted, feeling
stronger with every rhyme. Somehow he regained his balance. Just as Doc walked a thin line between helpless sobriety and incapacitated inebriation if he wished to act at
all, so Roger had to believe exactly enough to beat the wave
without getting sucked into the surfer mystique.

"Neat, feet, last, blast!" he chanted. Yeah, he was surfing now! But he was Roger, from Earth, who had spent
most of his adult life in public relations, who just happened
to be surfing atop the biggest killer groovy monster wave
that had ever existed!

He caught a familiar flash of color out of that same eye-
corner. The Mumbler was getting closer. A moment later,
he didn't even have to turn his head to see his rival surfer.
The Mumbler, hunched forward on his board, was passing
Roger by!

Roger told himself it didn't matter. He wasn't going to

buy into this surfing duel stuff, anyway. So the Mumbler reached the beach first—so what?

"Beach, reach," Roger mumbled distractedly. "Duel, fool."

The Mumbler would reach the beach first? That would never do. It was only now that Roger realized how meaningless his life had been until this moment. Winning was everything! He would be the hero of the beach, his greatest triumph ever!

He had to keep up that surfing! And even more than before, he had to do it with music!

This time, when Roger started to sing, the wave seemed somehow quieter, as if out of respect.

> "The Mad Mumbler better watch his skin,
> 'Cause this boy knows he's here to win.
> Roger proves he ain't no faddy,
> He'll blow away this here ho-daddy!"

They could hear him on the beach! He could see them clapping along! He laughed as the Cowabunga-munga produced a special swell just beneath his board, propelling him swiftly past the leather-suited surfer. Without a song, the Mad Mumbler didn't have a chance!

Roger sang another verse to complete the musical justice:

> "Roger's really goin' for that ride;
> The Cowabunga-munga's on his side!
> Now we know that revenge is sweet,
> And Roger, he wins by twenty feet!"

Roger's board glided onto the beach a goodly distance before the Mumbler as the Cowabunga-munga retreated out to sea.

The surfers converged on him as he stepped from his board. Bix Bale and the Belltones led with a furious surfing beat as the song went on forever:

"Oh, Roger's proved that he's the best;
He passed the Cowabunga test;
That guy can surf on anything;
Yeah, he's now the surfer king!"

The surfers lifted Roger onto their shoulders and propelled him into the crowd. He saw the Mumbler surf safely into shore as he was raised aloft. Even the leather-suited challenger cheered Roger—in his usual indistinct fashion—as the celebration really began.

Roger looked down on the adoring masses beneath him. He was king of the surfers. Everyone was dancing. Roger's life was fulfilled.

Among those who danced by were people Roger recognized: Zabana, Prince of the Jungle; Officer O'Clanrahan; Dwight the Wonder Dog.

People who did more than surf.

There were other things to life besides surfing?

Roger felt himself distancing himself from those ever-present guitar chords as he shook off the surfing spell once more. The music could no longer hold him as he watched a conga line of Doctor Dread, Menge the Merciless, and Professor Peril. Every one he recognized reminded him there was more at stake here than winning a surfing duel! He had to win the entire Cineverse!

"Hey!" everybody shouted. Bif BOOM bif BOOM boom boom boom de boom, the drums replied.

But how could he succeed? Sure, he'd triumphed over a monster wave, but that was nothing compared with the fates of myriad movie worlds. And things were changing even as he considered what to do next. Perhaps that had been his problem ever since he had gotten here—the Cineverse never stood still long enough for him to make a decision. Far to the west, over the ocean, the sun was sinking toward the horizon. He knew what sunsets meant, too—on this particular movie world, they were approaching The End. That's how surfing movies often ended, with everyone dancing up a storm.

But what did The End mean for all of them, good guys and bad guys? He'd never stayed on a world in the Cineverse long enough to see the conclusion of a plot. Now that he'd won the surfing duel, would they all dance like this forever?

That's when he saw Delores again. She was dancing too, but she didn't look happy about it. Perhaps it was because of her two partners, Mort the Killer Robot, and Diablo, the Gorilla with the Mind of a Man! The two dancing villains were taking turns, grabbing Delores' arms and twirling her about. It took Roger only a second to realize she was a dancer in distress!

Roger jumped down from the arms of the celebrating surfers. He had to be more than the greatest surfer on the beach. He had to save Delores and everyone else from the clutches of Doctor Dread!

But how to do it? He was one man, up against the amassed evil of the Cineverse. But, as he thought of it, he realized that the Cineverse, and the Cowabunga-munga, might have already shown him the way. Maybe, with song, all things were possible.

"Hit it, Bix!" he yelled, and the Belltones took it from the top as Roger sang along:

> "Is he threatening Delores?
> He's extinct as brontosaurus!
> Yeah, he's gone just like a gunshot,
> Farewell Mort the Killer Robot!"

And Mort the Killer Robot had disappeared before the crowd could say "Hey!" Still dancing, Diablo, the Gorilla with the Mind of a Man, looked at Roger and snarled. Roger answered with another verse:

> "Well, he's still dancing with Delores,
> But he's gone well before the chorus,

More forgotten than sarsaparilla,
Is Diablo with Mind-of-Man Gorilla!''

The gorilla vanished even more quickly than his metallic
companion before him.

Roger grinned and turned to Doctor Dread, his vocal
chords throbbing with a new-found power.

"Now, now, let's not do anything"—Dread paused uncertainly—"hasty."

"What has that do-gooder done?" Professor Peril wailed.
"Where will I ever again find cohorts so economical?"

"Pardon me for interrupting," Menge mentioned, "but
perhaps it would be better to ask these questions somewhere
else?"

"But you don't understand!" Peril went on, quite beside
himself. "Job opportunities are so limited for killer robots
and gorillas with brain transplants, they work for almost
nothing!"

"Bertha, if you would"—Dread paused in his directions—"escort our distraught compatriot, we will depart
until we discover some more"—another brief but discernible pause—"advantageous circumstance for our next meeting?"

But Roger wasn't going to let them go that easily.

"Come on, Bix!" he yelled. "Let's get 'em!"

Roger concentrated as he sang. He wanted this new rhyme
to be a killer!

"That Doctor Dread, he is awfully smug—" he began.

"Minions!" Dread yelled. "To my side!"

"But you know his grave's already dug—" Roger added.

"You have not seen the last of—" Dread paused menacingly.

"His time round here is not that long—" Roger continued, undaunted.

"This is not the time for menacing pauses!" Dread exclaimed hurriedly. "See you in the funny papers!"

The blue smoke showed up before Roger could complete his rhyme.

"And Doctor Dread and his gang are gone!" he finished anyway. The Belltones gave him a drum roll as everybody cheered.

Delores ran to him first. "Roger! That was magnificent!"

He took her in his arms. They kissed. Roger had no idea how long it had been since they had kissed; in a place like the Cineverse, it was probably impossible to tell anyway. It didn't matter. Any time at all without Delores was far too long.

They had to breathe eventually.

"I simply figured out a little bit about how the Cineverse works," he explained when he could talk again.

Everybody who was gathered around them cheered. And everybody was gathered around them. Roger almost blushed. He was the center of attention—no longer the sidekick he had been considered in the Western movie world. He wished, though, that he might discuss his heroics with Delores someplace that was a bit more private.

"Yes, but it comes to you so naturally!" Delores enthused, not letting Roger get away with his modesty. "It would be much more difficult for us in the Cineverse to rhyme so quickly. Why, people attend Hero School for years and aren't half as good!"

Everybody cheered again.

"So," Big Louie asked, "what do we do now?"

Roger glanced over at the sidekick, who shrugged apologetically.

"Simply moving the plot along," Louie explained.

"As you should," Roger agreed as he gently let go of Delores. "But I have things to tell you—"

"We'll talk as soon as we can," Delores agreed. "But Doctor Dread is certainly plotting his revenge even now. We still need to find Captain Crusader and save the Cine-

verse. After that, we can attend to''—it was Delores' turn
to pause as she glanced wistfully at Roger—''other things.''

Roger felt himself blushing again. Actually, he had been
thinking of talking about the Plotmaster, but now that Delores mentioned it . . . well . . . He cleared his throat, which
at least seemed a little more heroic.

Delores continued, her voice now brusquely official: ''We
came to this world with a specific purpose—not to find you,
dear Roger, but because this was the most likely whereabouts of Captain Crusader. Now, however, he seems to be
nowhere around. Think, Roger! Have you seen anyone who
could be the hero among heroes?''

Captain Crusader? Roger frowned. So—in a way—they
had both been on the same errand.

''No,'' he replied after a moment's reflection, ''but I
know somebody who can help us.'' If Captain Crusader
was somewhere in the vicinity, he was still hiding. But
Roger *had* thought of Dr. Davenport, and the astonishing
resources of her Institute of Very Advanced Science. There,
he knew, was one place that had the resources to find Captain
Crusader.

''We could go there, but—'' He stopped himself mid-
sentence when he remembered the crisis on the Advanced
Science world with VERA the computer. What if Dr. Davenport was still in trouble on her home world? He didn't
want to go from the relative safety of the surfing world to
a place so potentially risky to his allies and himself. But
they had to find Captain Crusader now. Doctor Dread was
already too powerful!

That's when Roger realized there might be another way.
It was highly experimental, of course, and, in attempting
it, he would have to test the limits of the power of surf
music, but maybe he could get Movie Magic to work for
him!

''But maybe,'' he added aloud, ''I can bring her here.''

''How?'' Delores asked.

"With the help of Bix Bale and the Belltones," he replied. "Hit it, guys!"

Roger sang, hoping against hope that his gamble would work:

> "Life on this beach is pretty neat,
>   The sun and surf almost complete;
>   But where's the laughter of young Dee Dee?
>   I long to hear her go—"

He stopped.

"—tee hee hee!" came a familiar laugh from the back of the crowd.

"It worked!" Roger yelled triumphantly.

"What worked?" Delores asked doubtfully.

"Dee Dee!" Roger called.

"You rang?" a perky voice called back.

"Who rang?" Delores asked. "Roger, are you sure—" But Roger only nodded.

"Come on over, Dee Dee!"

"Tee hee hee!" The pert beach bunny in the psychedelic green bikini jogged towards them through the crowd.

"This is your solution?" Delores asked gently.

"Exactly!" Roger replied. "This is Doctor Dee Dee Davenport, of the Institute of Very Advanced Science!"

"Tee hee hee," Dee Dee agreed. She waved at everybody as she trotted into their midst.

"Doctor Davenport?" Delores asked tentatively, offering her hand.

Dee Dee squealed with delight. She shook Delores' hand, her whole body bursting with energy. "Tee hee hee," she added.

Delores glanced at Roger. "The Institute of Very Advanced Science?"

"Well," Roger began. "I know it doesn't look quite—"

"Roger," Delores replied, her voice still far too gentle.

"How do I tell you this? Sometimes, people can be out in the sun too long—"

"But, no!" Roger objected. "She may be a cute and perky beach bunny here—"

"Tee hee hee," Dee Dee demonstrated.

"But on her home world she heads the Institute—"

"Personality change," Zabana, Prince of the Jungle, observed. "Like Doctor Dread."

"Roger—" Delores replied, the exasperation rising in her voice. "Would someone shut up that dog?"

"Yip, yip, bark!"

Roger hadn't noticed it before, but it was true. Dwight was going crazy.

"Bark, yip, yip!"

"Dwight says—" Louie began.

"In a moment, Louie," Delores interrupted. "So Dee Dee here heads a scientific institute—"

"—that I think can be instrumental in finding Captain Crusader!" Roger said rather more loudly than he should have. He was becoming a bit exasperated himself.

Dwight started barking all over again. Roger would have glanced over at the dog himself, but something large had risen in the sand directly in front of him.

"Please do not raise your voice to the woman who is to be my bride," the thing covered by sand announced.

"What is this?" Roger asked, his voice still not as quiet as it could have been.

"Arf, arf, bark!" Dwight interjected.

"Oh," Delores explained, "that's the Slime Monster."

The pile of sand introduced himself. "My friends call me Edward."

"And you're questioning the company that I keep?" Roger demanded.

"Tee hee hee," Dee Dee laughed appreciatively.

"I don't think jokes are appropriate on my future bride's behalf," the slime monster commented.

"What?" Roger was becoming even more incensed. "What's this future bride stuff?"

"Arf, bark, yip!" Dwight was getting frantic.

Delores threw up her hands. "Roger, this wasn't my idea."

"Not your idea?" He waved at the mobile pile of sand. "I suppose this guy just swept you off your feet?"

"And I find you cavorting with a beach bunny!" Delores snapped back.

Dee Dee stepped between them.

"Tee hee hee," she began apologetically. "It's time to cool it, guys. Remember, when you go to the beach, don't leave courtesy behind!"

Everybody stopped and stared at the beach bunny. Roger wondered if everyone was thinking the same thing he was:

What Dee Dee had just said sounded like something that should be said by the hero among heroes.

"Bark, yip, bark!" Dwight announced with finality.

"Exactly!" Louie replied.

"Captain Crusader!" Delores and Roger exclaimed together.

"So nice of you to—reveal yourself," a particularly oily voice said from the midst of the crowd.

There was a small explosion. Dee Dee clutched at her firm and perky stomach.

"Tee—" she gasped. "Tee hee—"

"She's been shot!" Delores yelled.

Dee Dee/Captain Crusader nodded as she swayed back and forth, both hands over her wound.

"Remember," she replied between clenched teeth, "a bullet takes—only a minute, but a—friend is yours—for life." She toppled forward, onto the sand.

Doctor Dread and Menge the Merciless, now in their more traditional bad guy costumes, stepped forward from the crowd.

"Menge, that shot was"—Dread paused triumphantly—

"excellent. How easily they fell for our little"—this time he simultaneously paused and gloated—"ruse."

Menge's reply was more to the point:

"Ah hahahaha. Ah hahahaha!"

⌒ 18 ⌒
"The Fateful Moment!"

Captain Crusader? Shot?

Roger realized at last that this must be the life-or-death situation the Plotmaster had spoken of!

"You'll pay for this!" Roger shouted with upraised fist.

"He's beginning to sound like a hero," Menge replied smoothly. "Righteous indignation with absolutely no originality whatsoever."

"Kill!" Zabana yelled with jungle-bred determination.

"Pitiful fools!" Menge crowed. "You will, of course, permit us to gloat over our accomplishments."

"Shoot!" Doc staggered to his feet as he pulled his six-gun and tried to sober himself to the task at hand.

"How—clever of us," Dread agreed smugly. "To seemingly disappear, only to—reposition ourselves!"

"Arrest!" Officer O'Clanrahan pulled a nightstick and handcuffs free from his belt.

"And wait for the moment when you hopeless do-gooders revealed the one person who might have stopped us!" Menge smirked.

"Arf!" Dwight agreed with his fellows, animal bloodlust in his eyes.

"And now we have stopped—Captain Crusader." Dread chortled unpleasantly. "What do you say to that?"

"Slime!" Edward chorused, the sand-covered monster having the last word on the subject.

Delores stepped forward, and waved for the rest to follow her. She shouted her defiance to Dread and Menge:

"Now that you've shot Captain Crusader, everybody's going to be after you!"

"It is your death!" Zabana agreed.

"Well, maybe," Dread allowed, "—if we planned to stick around."

The blue smoke exploded around them.

"See you in the funny papers"—Dread hesitated with finality—"if we don't remove you first!"

And they were gone.

Roger knelt by Dr. Dee Dee Davenport.

"You really are Captain Crusader?"

She clutched her stomach as she grimaced in pain. Her bright green bikini was turning brown with blood. She nodded.

"Yes, I am the Captain."

"But why didn't you tell me?"

"I did tell you," she replied. "When you pointed the Ring of Truth at me. And then I changed the subject. The Ring of Truth does work, you know—at least for getting people to tell the truth. It's not that good for getting around the Cineverse, though." She took a shuddery breath. "A lot of things aren't working as well around here as they used to."

"You deceived me!" Roger exclaimed. "But why?"

Captain Crusader shrugged her shapely shoulders. "A hero has to be—flexible in times like these. Besides, you had to learn how to—be a hero, too."

The others gathered around Roger and the Captain.

"Dread gone," Zabana explained.

"Captain Crusader?" Louie asked. "How bad is—"

Dee Dee tried to smile, but the pain was all too evident. She took another ragged breath.

"I can last—for another page or two. I have to—to tell you everything you need to know." She reached out and weakly patted Roger's hand. "Your coming to the Cineverse—that was partly my doing, you know. We needed someone from outside, someone who could see beyond the separate movie worlds, someone who could work by my side. Too bad it came—too late."

"It may not be too late!" Roger insisted. "Maybe we can get help."

Dee Dee shook her head. "No—I'm a goner. That's one of the things that a hero always knows. Forgive me—for not showing myself to you sooner, but you had to learn how to control the Cineverse—like you learned how to control the Cowabunga-munga!"

She coughed then, covering her mouth with her hand. When she stopped, there was a discreet amount of blood on her palm.

"Captain Crusader?" Officer O'Clanrahan wailed, beside himself with grief. "Dying?"

"What'll we do now?" Doc chorused.

"I may be dying," Dee Dee agreed, "but there'll always be a Captain Crusader. It's one of the Laws of the Cineverse." She looked up at the man from Earth, her bright blue eyes alive with purpose. "Now, Roger, it'll have to be you."

"Me?" Roger objected. "But—"

"I'm sorry—but you have no choice." She clenched her teeth as she shivered with pain. "It is too bad—that I did not have the time—to properly train you. But you are the only one here—with the proper raw materials—the only one—who can stand up to Doctor Dread."

Her eyelids fluttered. "Take my hand, Roger. It's getting dark!"

Roger did as she asked.

"Remember," she said, her voice barely a whisper, "a song—in your heart—and a smile on—your lips—keeps Old Man—Trouble—away."

Her breath left her in a rush. Her hand went limp in Roger's. Her eyes closed. She was gone.

"Ssrrffmm." The Mumbler added his incoherent condolences.

"I suppose," Edward intoned morosely, "an event like this means it would be improper to announce our engagement—just yet."

But Delores was beyond caring about the Slime Monster's intentions. "Captain Crusader?" she whispered, as if she could barely say the words. "Gone? What can we do?"

Roger laid the Captain's hand gently upon the sand, then stood and turned to look at all the others.

"Just what she told us to do," he replied. "We will carry on, until we defeat Doctor Dread!"

Roger wished he felt as confident as he sounded. He didn't know the first thing about fighting Doctor Dread, unless he could do it by firing off press releases. He didn't even know his way around the Cineverse. How could he possibly hope to defeat the forces of evil of every movie world that ever existed?

The more he thought about it, the more it seemed impossible. He was the new Captain Crusader? The Cineverse was doomed. What could possibly be any worse?

"Look!" Frankie yelled from behind Roger. "Captain Crusader! She's gone!"

Roger spun around. He looked where Dee Dee's body had been. There was nothing there now but an indentation in the sand.

The wind had started up again along the beach. Seagulls called to each other in the sky.

Big Louie shook Roger's elbow.

"Roger! Something's happening! I can feel it!"

There was an explosion, followed by blue smoke.

"Roger!" a woman's voice shouted indignantly. "What

have you done? What is the meaning of this?''

Roger knew that voice. It *could* get worse, after all.

The blue smoke cleared, revealing a very unhappy and somewhat overdressed woman of middle years.

It was his mother.

"Well?" she said in that you'd-better-have-an-explanation-or-else voice she had honed through years of experience. "Are you going to answer me?"

"What's the meaning of what, Mother?" Roger replied, automatically adopting his most conciliatory tone.

It was, of course, the absolute wrong tone to use on one's mother.

"Don't act innocent with me, young man!" Surfers scattered as she strode purposefully across the sand toward her son. "There is something going on here, and I demand to know what it is!"

Roger looked around at Zabana, Doc, and Louie, still in their double-breasted suits, and Delores with her spangled evening gown. Then, of course, there was his own very soggy jogging suit, and almost everybody else wearing surfing duds. And his mother wanted him to explain all this?

"Mother," Roger replied at last, hoping against hope that she would accept his answer, "it's better if you don't know."

"Roger Aloysius Gordon!" His mother declared in a tone suitable for declaring World War III.

"Aloysius?" Louie asked.

"Family name," Roger replied. "Never used."

Except, he thought rather than said, when his mother was in one of *those* moods.

And his mother had only begun. "First, you disappear. Heaven knows, you never call me in the first place, so how would I *know* when you disappear? But this time you decided you were too busy to go to work, too. The office was calling all over the place, looking for you. They even called Susan—she was always such a nice girl—I don't see why the two of you ever split up. She at least took the time to call me. I tell you, we were both worried sick."

Susan? Roger thought about objecting. After all, he and Susan had gotten divorced years ago. Not that his mother noticed. She was happy as long as Susan called.

"And then I couldn't find Mr. M!" his mother continued melodramatically. "His house was deserted, his little red sports car gone. I tell you, it felt like people were disappearing right and left in my life. You don't know how insecure that can make a person."

Roger nodded. Susan or no Susan, it was too late to object. He knew his mother's tirades—they grew longer every time you tried to let her know there was more than one side to an issue. The only way anyone could possibly survive was to suffer in silence.

"Well, what could I do?" His mother sighed, a faraway look in her eyes. "With you gone—it's funny. I started to think how you were as a little boy—I mean, besides being messy and inconsiderate. I started going through my keepsake drawer. You know how sentimental a mother can be. And then I found this cheap plastic ring."

She looked up wistfully, including everyone on the beach in her conversation. "You know, when Roger was a boy, he loved the free prizes that came in cereal boxes. It seemed I had saved one, along with those old school reports and handmade valentines."

Big Louie had sidled up to Roger. He stood on his tiptoes and whispered in Roger's ear. "She'll go on like this for quite a while, won't she?"

Roger nodded, his eyes still respectfully watching his lecturing parent.

"And then there was all this blue smoke. At first, I thought it was the furnace, backing up again—"

"Did you ever think about the implications of all this," Louie went on. "Your mother not only accidentally uses the Captain Crusader Decoder Ring, but she ends up here, in the exact same place as her son? Do you realize how coincidental this all is?"

Roger nodded even more vehemently. Of course, after what he'd been through in the Cineverse, nothing would surprise him.

"No, nothing surprises me, either," Louie agreed, even though Roger hadn't spoken aloud. "But this is still too strange to be coincidence. I sense the hand of the Plotmaster in all this."

"The Plotmaster?" Roger asked, his voice a mixture of astonishment and relief. At last he could tell the others what had happened to him! "I've met the Plotmaster!"

Everybody—with the exception of Roger's mother, who was too busy complaining—stopped to stare at Roger.

"What?" Delores asked gently, a look of concern in her deep blue eyes. "Are you sure?"

"Plotmaster mythic," the jungle prince added. "Even more mythic than Zabana!"

"Nobody ever actually meets the Plotmaster," Louie agreed as he shook his head in admiration. "Maybe you do have methods!"

"Roger?" his mother demanded. "Are you listening to me?"

"In a minute, Mother." Roger turned back to the others. "But a number of us have spoken to the Plotmaster. He saw not only me, but Louie, Doc, and Zabana!"

"He did?" Louie asked incredulously.

"Shure!" Doc scoffed from his spot on the ground. "And they call me the town drunk!"

"No, wait!" Roger insisted. He had to get them to believe him. He had the feeling this whole thing with the Plotmaster was somehow tied up with the Change, and the very fate of the Cineverse! But how could he explain it?

"It was after we got caught in that Cineverse cycle," he began, "—you know, all those swashbucklers."

"Swashbucklers?" Zabana asked, the oddest look on his jungle-bred features.

"And then he came and rescued us," Roger added rapidly. "But he said that none of us would—uh—remember any of it."

His voice faltered as he realized the problem with his explanation. How could anybody remember what happened if they weren't supposed to?

His mother's voice cut into the silence. "Roger, if you're not going to pay attention to me, I might as well leave." She glanced up and down the beach with a frown, as if this was the first time she had really looked at her surroundings. "How did I get here, anyway?"

The jungle prince spoke hesitantly. "Zabana . . . remember . . . swords."

"Mrs. Gordon," Delores said helpfully, "we'll try to explain everything to you, as soon as we can figure it out ourselves."

"Well, thank you," Roger's mother replied, somewhat mollified. "At least someone is looking out for my welfare. And who is this attractive young lady? For heaven's sake, Roger, you could introduce people to your mother!"

"In a minute, Mother," Roger answered. "So you remember the Plotmaster, too?"

Zabana nodded slowly. "Only now you mention it."

"Yeah," Louie added slowly. "I remember—all these swashbuckling places—and this guy in blue smoke."

"Blue shmoke?" Doc called from the sand. "I thought it wash one of my vishions!"

Louie whistled. "And Roger remembered it. See, guys? I told you Roger had his methods!"

"No wonder he new Captain Crusader," Zabana agreed.

Oh, that. In all the hubbub with his mother, Roger had almost forgotten the new honor bestowed upon him. But the more he thought of it—even if he could somehow become the hero's hero—this situation was too serious for a lone individual. Combating the Change called for everybody working together. He decided he'd have to have a heart-to-heart talk with everybody about this, too—as soon as he cleared up this business about the Plotmaster.

"But there's more," Roger continued. "The Plotmaster contacted me for a reason. There was something he wanted to warn me about."

"Roger!" his mother exclaimed, the imperious tone returning to her voice. "I'll start warning you, if you don't introduce me—"

"In a minute—" Roger began, when he realized he was surrounded by blue smoke. He glanced around at the fog-shrouded shapes of his companions, shapes that had ceased moving, as if the smoke had frozen the world. There was something else odd, too. This smoke had arrived without the usual explosion. But there was some sound— music, faint and high, like a distant choir of angels. Who could—

ROGER, BABY.
LONG TIME NO SEE!
WE HAVE TO TALK.

It was, of course, the Plotmaster, backlit as usual, smoking his blue-smoke cigar. This time, Roger was considerably happier to see him.

"At last!" Roger called. He grinned broadly. The Plotmaster could explain everything. "Now you can finish your warning. I do appreciate it, sir. I'm sure it helped me to survive. But could you tell me, was it something to do with the Art Film world, or was it about the size of the Cowabunga-munga?"

But the Plotmaster shook his backlit head.

ROGER, SWEETIE, BABY!
MY WARNING WAS FOR NOTHING THAT
COMMON.
THOSE THINGS HAPPEN IN THE CINEVERSE
EVERY DAY.

Of course. Roger should have realized that. After all, the Plotmaster hadn't meddled in most of the earlier crises they had faced. The situation would have to be truly extraordinary for this powerful being to show his hand. That, of course, meant the warning could have referred to only one thing.

"Oh, then it was the death of Captain Crusader," Roger said with confidence.

But the Plotmaster's head was still shaking.

NO, EVEN AN EVENT OF THAT SCOPE
IS NOT UNUSUAL IN THE CINEVERSE.
LISTEN, THIS IS IMPORTANT.

The Plotmaster took a long drag on his cigar, as if contemplating what was the best way to broach a subject of this gravity. Blue smoke curled upwards to join the like-colored fog that surrounded the two of them, obscuring everything else on the beach. After a moment, the big man waved his stogie at Roger.

WE'RE TALKING ABOUT REAL DISASTER, HERE.
I HAVE TO TALK TO YOU BEFORE YOUR
MOTHER SHOWS UP.

"My mother?" Roger asked, almost laughing despite himself. What would the Plotmaster want with his mother. "But she's here already."

SHE IS?

The Plotmaster stood there, frozen for an instant, as if he couldn't believe what he had just heard.

A chill shot through Roger. The mention of his mother didn't seem humorous anymore. This was the first time he had ever heard fear in the big man's voice.

The Plotmaster looked upwards.

SID, DID YOU HEAR THAT?
WHY WASN'T I TOLD?

Roger couldn't make out the answer. It sounded like nothing so much as a blast of music from the angelic choir.

SID, THAT'S NO EXCUSE!
I DON'T CARE ABOUT YOUR CHERUBS!
YOU'RE FIRED.

The angelic choir cut off abruptly. The Plotmaster turned his attention back to Roger.

LIKE I TOLD YOU, ROGER BABY, I CAN BE
RUTHLESS.
BUT WHAT CAN WE DO—NOW?

He picked up a thick sheaf of paper from the table behind him, and began to leaf through it. Roger remembered: Last time, the Plotmaster had called this wad of paper "the script."

UM

the Plotmaster muttered,

WELL IF THAT'S TRUE, MAYBE WE CAN—

He turned the page.

UH-OH.

He flipped a few more pages.

OH DEAR.
OH NO.
THAT'S INHUMAN.

He sighed, and looked at the end.
He didn't move for a long moment. The blue ember at

the end of his cigar dimmed and threatened to go out. The last page had left him speechless. He threw the script back on the table, then turned heavily back to Roger, as if he had the weight of the Cineverse upon him.

I'M SORRY, ROGER.
I DID TRY TO REACH YOU BEFORE IT WAS—
TOO LATE.

Then there was another sound. It wasn't an angelic choir this time. The noise was a harsh, staccato braying, like the laughter of some demented god.

The Plotmaster threw his hands in front of his face, as if to ward off some invisible danger. He screamed at Roger over the booming laugh:

OH NO!
THE CHANGE HAS BEGUN!
I CAN DO NO MORE!

MORE!
More!
more!
more.

The Plotmaster was gone, the blue smoke drifting away. The echo faded as Roger realized people were once again moving around him. His mother was complaining again, but everyone else had turned to stare at a spot farther down the beach.

And, Roger realized, the laughter hadn't gone away.

⟩ **19** ⟨

"The Change—or the End?"

"Ah hahahaha!" Menge the Merciless chortled from where he stood in front of a gigantic silver machine. "Ah hahahaha!"

"Why, Mr. M!" Roger's mother called. "What a pleasant surprise!"

Menge stopped laughing. "Mrs. G. What are you doing here?"

"A woman has to travel," she replied. "It's so important to travel, Mr. M. Especially when you reach our age."

Roger couldn't believe this! His mother was flirting with one of the most evil men in the Cineverse!

"But, Mother!" he interrupted. "Don't you realize who this is? This is Menge the Merciless!"

His mother looked quizzically at Dread's henchman.
"Mr. M?"

"Alas, Mrs. G.," Menge said with a sad nod, "your son is quite correct."

"Oh, Mr. M!" Roger's mother said with a smile.

"You're always so polite. Roger, you could learn a lesson from him."

"Mother!" Roger insisted.

"And who, exactly, is Menge the Merciless?" his mother added with the same polite smile.

"He criminal!" Zabana ventured.

"One of the foulest fiends in the Cineverse!" Big Louie added helpfully.

"Dear lady," Menge added smoothly. "All this, too, is correct."

Roger's mother dimpled at being called "dear lady."

"Oh, Mr. M.," she said enthusiastically, "I'm sure there's some way we can work this out."

Roger couldn't believe this. "Mother! Don't you understand? Menge the Merciless is a supervillain!"

She turned to Roger with a frown.

"Now, now, Roger. When a woman gets to be my age, she can't be that choosy."

"Well, we'll have to talk about that later, Mrs. G." Menge interjected pleasantly. He patted the complicated machine he had brought with him. "In the meantime, I have to fry your son with the Zeta Ray."

"Oh, dear," his mother replied, a bit of worry creeping in. "Will it hurt him?"

"Not physically, no." Menge replied. "You see, I work for an organization that is intent upon taking over the Cineverse—the area that you are now visiting. As a part of this, we have already removed our primary obstacle, one Captain Crusader. However, we have since detected a great surge of energy in this particular area, and realized that there might be other threats—however minor—that we should dispense with so that our conquest will be that much easier. We have determined that your son, Mrs. G., may be one of these minor threats."

Roger's mother's hands fluttered in front of her breast. "Do you know, Mr. M., that's the first real explanation

I've had since I've gotten here!'' She glanced reprovingly at her son. ''If only everyone could be as polite. Still, I don't think I can agree to let you point something potentially harmful at my son—even though he is sometimes thought-less.''

''Oh, I assure you, Mrs. G.,'' Menge replied quickly, ''he won't feel a thing.'' He pointed at the twin fins, large enough to adorn a 1959 Buick, that sprouted from either side of the large silver contraption. ''The special evil-con-ductors contained in the vacuum tubes of the Zeta Ray will—within a matter of seconds—subtly alter the alpha patterns within your son's brain. In that selfsame matter of seconds, his whole attitude will change. He will no longer be a worthless, namby-pamby do-gooder. He will suddenly see the justice of our cause!''

''Oh, you men and your technical explanations!'' Mrs. G. giggled. ''Still—''

''I guarantee,'' Menge continued, ''that—after the ray is used—he will also be much more polite.''

''My. Really?'' Roger's mother nodded, obviously im-pressed. ''Well, in that case—''

Menge, still smiling, reached for a button on the side of the silver machine, a button labeled with the usual large cardboard sign: ZETA CONTROL.

When Menge looked away, Zabana leapt for him.

''You no zap Roger!'' the jungle prince exclaimed. ''Za-bana zap Zeta!''

There was a brief, unequal struggle. Menge was picked up by jungle-bred muscles and thrown roughly against the machine, his elbow hitting the Zeta button.

''Bunga bonga blooie!'' the prince of the jungle cried.

Zabana closed in on the supervillain, ready for the kill.

There was a crackling noise. The machine jerked as Menge and Zabana grappled.

''Run!'' Louie shouted. ''The thing's gonna go off!''

Almost everybody ran. The crackling turned into a loud, whooping sound, and a yellow ray shot forth, bathing the only person who hadn't run—Roger's mother—in golden light!

"What's happening?" Roger yelled. "Mother!"

Zabana grabbed a fistful of wiring from the silver gizmo's undercarriage. He yanked it free. The ray cut off abruptly.

"Oh, dear," Mrs. G. remarked. "I feel so different. Hee." She placed a hand delicately over her mouth. "Hee hee. Heeheeheehee!" She began to laugh uncontrollably.

Menge the Merciless had managed to free himself from Zabana's grip. He ran a few feet away, nodding grimly as he retreated.

"The Zeta Ray has done its hellish work."

Hellish work? Roger looked back to his laughing mother. What could Menge mean by that?

"Mother—" he began again.

His mother turned to look at him, and showed a smile Roger had never seen before. No, this was not the smile of a loving mother. It was not even the grim smile of a mother about to administer a paddling. It was, instead, a smile of pure evil!

When she spoke at last, her voice was low and full of menace. "We'll teach sons to ignore their mothers! Hee-heehee! Heeheehee!"

Menge the Merciless ran to her side.

"Yes!" he cried triumphantly. "But not now! You have to destroy him by surprise, when he least expects it!"

Mrs. G. frowned petulantly. "Why?"

"It's much more"—he hesitated in the finest style of Dr. Dread—"evil that way."

The nasty grin returned to her face. "Of course! Why didn't I think of that?" She clapped her hands. "This is going to be so much fun! Hee hee hee heeheehee!"

"Oh, Mrs. G! Together, we will rule the Cineverse! Ah hahahaha! Ah hahahaha!"

Menge took her hand in his.

"See you in the funny papers!" he cried.

There was the usual blue smoke.

"Oh, dear," Delores said softly. "Oh, Roger."

Roger didn't say anything.

His mother? A villain?

The Plotmaster was right.

This was terrible! How could it get any worse?

"Roger!" Delores yelled.

"Roger," Edward the Slime Monster repeated in a determined voice. "The engagement is over."

"The engagement is over?" Roger repeated, only half listening. "Well, at least that's good news."

"I'm glad you're taking it so well," Edward added solemnly. "No hard feelings."

"Roger!" Delores insisted.

Roger glanced up from where he had been moodily studying the sand. Now that Roger noticed, wasn't the Slime Monster holding Delores a bit too tightly?

"Hey!" he yelled. "What are you doing?"

"We are leaving," Edward explained patiently. He glanced distractedly at the woman who struggled in his grip.

"Oh, dear," he added, a hint of apology in his voice. "Perhaps you misunderstood. I am unused to talking with humans. I am much more used to covering them with slime. But I told you the engagement was over. Delores and I will be married tonight."

"ROGER!" There seemed to be a growing panic in Delores' voice.

"Tonight?" Roger asked, thoroughly confused once more. "But I thought, what with the search for Captain Crusader, and our cause and all, you had decided to postpone—"

"That was before the Change," Edward interrupted.

"The Change?" Roger repeated in a whisper.

The Slime Monster nodded its muck-covered head. "Can't you feel it? Captain Crusader gone, Menge the Merciless triumphant, your mother Zeta-rayed into a life of evil. The delicate balance of the Cineverse is gone. The Change is upon us again. The Cineverse as we know it will soon cease to exist.''

Edward hugged Delores even closer to his chest.

"Even you would not deny a slime monster his last few moments of wedded bliss, would you?''

Roger realized then that he had been wrong again. It could still get worse, and was in fact getting worse with every passing moment. If he did not act quickly, he was going to lose the love of his life to a Slime Monster!

"But—'' he began. But what? How did you reason with a creature composed of muck?

"Zabana say attack!'' the jungle prince exclaimed.

Maybe, Roger realized, Zabana was right. They were many, the monster only one. Maybe you couldn't reason with a Slime Monster. Maybe, if they moved quickly enough, and they attacked all at once, they could overwhelm the Slime Monster. Maybe—

"If you insist,'' Edward replied.

Roger only had a chance to take one step forward before it got worse than it had ever been before.

Only one step, and he was covered with slime.

"*ROGER!*'' Delores screamed a final time.

But then the muck rose to cover his ears, and he heard no more.

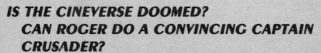

IS THE CINEVERSE DOOMED?
CAN ROGER DO A CONVINCING CAPTAIN CRUSADER?
WHAT DOES HIS MOTHER WANT FROM HIM, ANYWAY?
AND WHERE IN THE CINEVERSE WOULD A SLIME MONSTER GO FOR A HONEY-MOON?

ALL THIS AND MORE WILL BE ANSWERED IN
THE DYNAMIC CONCLUSION:

REVENGE OF THE FLUFFY BUNNIES

Coming Soon, to a bookstore
in YOUR neighborhood!

249